The
RAPE of
BHUDEVI

The RAPE of BHUDEVI

iAnand

PARTRIDGE
A Penguin Random House Company

To order additional copies of this book, contact
Partridge India
000 800 10062 62
www.partridgepublishing.com/india
orders.india@partridgepublishing.com

'O Opportunity, thy guilt is great!
'Tis thou that executest the traitor's treason;
Thou Set'st the wolf where he the lamb may get;
Whoever plots the sin, thou 'point'st the season;
'Tis thou that spurn'st at right, at law, at reason;
And in thy shady cell, where none may spy him,
Sits Sin, to seize the souls that wander by him.

William Shakesphere, The Rape of Lucrece.
Source www.opensourceshakesphere.org

To Janaki, Raji and the newcomer,
for giving me the freedom to work on this book,
sacrificing their time with me.

CHAPTER 1

I looked at the current assignment. I had to probe into this abduction and possible rape thing. It was a sudden development. I mean my involvement with this abduction-rape. I looked at the email. I had to travel to Delhi, with all expenses paid.

I objected. It was supposed to be my holiday time. Hotels were booked, the transportation all arranged. Cancelling it would be expensive to me.

My boss Sugriv had already promised Raghav, that I would be on the task. Sugriv owed Raghav a lot. Raghav had helped Sugriv get hold of his company, during the hostile takeover bid by his brother. So he could not refuse Raghav, and he assured me that the company would bear all expenses.

So I re-jigged my itinerary. A few days in Delhi. Then to Bhimtal. The resort personnel were happy to accommodate my request. My change of itinerary in a busy season helped them satisfy some of the others in a queue, during the peak holiday season, and I too got a few extra days of the resort. And most important, the boss was happy.

Now my holiday plan was to laze in the resort overlooking the Naukuchiya tal (nine cornered lake). My friend had visited last year and told me that it was a good place, nice view, mountains, some paragliding, but nothing for him. He needed the hustle and bustle of a crowded place. To him, it was like, nothing to do.

Well, that's exactly what I planned to do during my holidays. Nothing! Suvi and I had got married last year, and I planned to be with and within her. And nothing else.

I had recently read about the "G Spot Hammer technique" and along with the variable ramp that I had purchased, I planned to explore this technique, along with some other techniques that were in backlog.

Now to answer who I am and what do I have to do with rape cases. I have nothing to do with rape cases. I am a mere cyber security personnel in KK Enterprises. My name is Anjani. We provide different cyber security services to some top clients. While most cyber security guys are just configuring their firewalls and installing the latest antivirus and anti-spyware software, we also do some snooping around. And once in a while, there is a need to do some leg work.

Now, to tell you that we are no small timers, we have a lot of software experts, and they make a lot of tools. I am kind of a Jack of all. A kind of handyman to Sugriv's enterprise.

At some point of time, I had this concept or idea of myself as a hacking guru. Do some ethical hacking, save some good dudes from the bad guys. However, now I am more of a handyman to Sugriv and his corporation. He hands over the important assignments to me and lets me run the business once in a while, when he is busy and then tells me how many mistakes I had made. However, he trusts me and I trust that he does all this for my own good. We are a small outfit but make some good profits in this business.

We typically get cases from parents eager to know if their daughter is being predated upon or what their children are up to. Sometimes a bank gets hacked, and they hand over some activity. Like searching who visited the cybercafé and stuff like that. Most of my time is spent filling up forms. You need information about a certain IP address that has violated the cyber laws. You have to fill up a number of forms. Get the information in e-documents and then fill more forms to get them out and then have to analyze and then once you have zoomed onto something, then the entire e-traces have to be returned, and we have to provide the analysis reports. Then the internet service provider would take some action against the culprit, if there is convincing evidence.

If the case is a child predator one, then the Internet service provider's IT team is very helpful. If it is from a grown up male or female, then they are more wary. Either way, I am left with filling a number of forms. I have many friends there, who would look up some urgent information and provide me with a clue if the person or persons are clean or there is something to fish around.

Sometimes it is some celebrity, who needs a firewall installed or some such small service and Sugriv may end up choosing me to do this kind of activity. I don my 'engineer's hat' and gladly do such tasks.

In my knowledge, cyber law violators generally get some off-the-shelf products to shield their activity. Use VPN or some other secure methods. We have sufficient tools to crack such secure codes. But there are some very sick professionals, who make their own codes, and then we have to make our own codes. They may use different methods to hide their tracks, and we use methods to trace these hidden tracks.

Some users think that they can go to a cybercafé and do stuff, and no one will notice or be able to trace them. Here we use legwork. Once we have traced a misuse to a cybercafé, we try to establish a pattern of the visits made there. And we will have one of our guys start going there as a regular, and once we get the criminal there at the same time as our personnel, then it is easier to crack the case.

Once I establish the trace, it is the legal department's headache to go to the police and file FIR's and handle the other legwork. This was a high-profile case. Bhudevi and Raghav were almost the first couple of India. Bhudevi was a good actress, rated among the very best in India and Raghav was a CEO of a large organization. RA incorporated!

I had to go to Delhi and get the details from Raghav's office. I thought that it must be some cyber activity like sending lewd messages or dirty chat or some dirty emails that needed to be traced. A week would be sufficient for the same. Any ways I am supposed to be lucky.

I mean lucky for others. Or as others say, I bring luck to them, or I complete their tasks in time. Some of my friends think that I am lucky to be where I am. Things seem to happen automatically in my favor. Or so they say. At least, that's what Sugriv told me while sending me on this mission. I also knew that if I handled this well, there could be a promotion coming my way. I was already number two and would remain number two forever, but the change in what people call me makes me and Suvi happy. Suvi gets bored with the title I have and thinks that I should be getting a fancier one.

The next thing was to inform Suvi about the change of plans. She was between jobs. So it was not much of a problem. She was worried and asked me if we had to pack more clothes.

"No, we will get our laundry done in Delhi, and so we will not have any issues."

"Do they use clean water? I have seen the Yamuna river, and it is not very clean. In fact, the TV reports say that the Yamuna is already urine water before it enters Delhi. What if they use the water from Yamuna?"

I quickly imagined a lot of Dhobhi's (laundrymen) washing our clothes on the banks of a dirty Yamuna river. Maybe Suvi thought this was what happened. The Dhobi's applying soap to our clothes and manually washing them with a brush or something. They have washing machines even in the poorest of homes, and people use clean potable municipal water to wash clothes.

"They get municipal water in the hotels and use this municipal water, which is as good as mineral water to wash clothes. It is drinkable water and the TV reports just raise some dust. Do not worry."

"OK." I could feel that she did not trust what I was saying.

When I reached home, there was one more bag, packed with extra clothes. She had also packed some extra detergent, and I was sure that she would be hand washing some of the clothes during our holiday.

5

Especially the undergarments. I had better pack some rope, just in case the hotel did not have a clothes-line to dry the hand-washed clothes. There is no sense in arguing about these things with women. You will again end up being the idiot of this town!

Suvi wanted to know why I was being asked to do this dirty job. She thought I would be coming in contact with criminals of the worst kind. I told her, that I had to do unearth some cyber tracks and that the task would be done sitting in an A/C office. Work hours would be low (at least I hoped so) and I would be home quite early in the evening.

"Why do you have to be involved with Rapists?"

"I don't have to be. I will only be doing some tracing of emails and finding the culprit."

"Still! Why you for this Rape case?" I did not bother to remind Suvi that it was an abduction and rape was only a possibility, at least as of now.

"It is because it is the fiancée of Raghav, who has been raped. I guess."

"That famous multibillionaire"

"And his fiancée Bhudevi."

"That Bhudevi! OK. I heard that they have a live-in relationship." In today's world, people did not get married like me and Suvi. We were part of the brigade trying to establish the old methods of living. Live-in's were also very rare. People did not like to commit to one person anymore. People had many partners, and many people had many cyber sex-droids living with them.

"Many do not believe in the institution of marriage or Live-in any more. So Sad!"

"What do you think of the rapist?"

"I do not know anything. In fact, I do not know who the rapist is. However, I will find out."

What did I think of rapists? Well, the word 'rape' incites memories of woman screaming and running around. And a man chasing her. Tearing her clothes, woman manages to escape. Man catches with her and some more running around.

In fact, come to think of it, the word reminds me of a group of men doing this with a single woman or girl. The woman or girl screaming, shouting for help. What a cacophony! I think all this comes from the many ancient, classical Hindi movies that I watch. Finally, the woman is shown with clothes tattered; some blood or tomato ketchup sprayed on her face and generally looking disheveled.

The act is not shown in Hindi movies. And the woman either commits suicide or seeks vengeance.

When I think of a rapist, I am also reminded of a scene from a movie wherein the girl is being chased by three or four villains, and next she screams, "Leave me for god's sake!" And the Villain says, "If I leave you for god, then am I to eat the Prasad. Who will fulfill my lust?" Prasad is some sweet offered as god's food or like the break soaked in water that is given in churches. Some punch line, that one . . .

In most Hindi, movies, the rapists are well to do people, preying upon a poor woman or girl.

The most famous or infamous actual rape was that of Nirbhaya in Delhi. The girl was raped and beaten to her ultimate death by four low lives. A minor teenager too involved in that. A bus driver and three more people did this in a running bus in the city. That shook the conscience of the people ultimately bringing the culprits to justice. However, that was a longtime ago.

There was also a case in the past where a girl was raped by a politician in a college in Mumbai, but since he was well connected in politics, he got away. That too a long time ago.

I cannot imagine why a man would rape a woman today. With so many women available to satisfy your lust and to top that, in this cyberdroid age, you could buy any number of cyber droids who offer a most wonderful experience at very low cost. In fact, hardened Sex-Droid users claim that the human-human sex era is coming to an end. So wonderful is the sex droid experience, that some claim that they no longer like having sex with another human.

I looked up for some literature on celebrity abduction and rape. I typed 'The Fan' and was suggested 'The Fan Club By Irving Wallace'. I went ahead with the search. This was a novel about some guys kidnapping a celebrity. Something similar to what we had in hand. It had been a best-seller and would be worth a read. Was it some crazed fan? Could it be possible that he had picked up the idea from this book? I put this link in my favorite searches.

But who did all these things nowadays? Ransom could make some sense, but people were generally well to do. Everybody has droids nowadays to satisfy lust. I could understand someone stealing a million-dollar Sex-Droid, because of the fantastic experience it was supposed to give as compared to a human or an ordinary sex-droid.

It must be some sick guy. I mean the kidnapper or rapist.

CHAPTER 2

Dashmukh or DM as people called him, had been a growing multibillionaire at that time. The first time he had seen her. He was running a successful adult movie production house and was looking for new talent. His talent hunt led him to Bhudevi. It was infatuation at first sight. She was 19 or 20 at that time.

He was turned on, just looking at her.

A breathlessness that he had never before experienced.

His throat parched.

He could not think of anything but her beautiful body.

His mind exploded with sexual thoughts and his body and organs responding to these thoughts.

That was then.

The world needs its DM's. Every now and then, the underworld grows strong. And somebody is needed to control it. DM entered the world in some kind of poverty. He toiled hard and studied harder. He achieved good grades and had a sharp intellect. Good men always saw, in him, somebody who could control the poor. He was always available to talk sense and get the job done. From his early teenage days, he always had a job supervising people. Having been born poor, he was very compassionate towards the poor on one hand and became hard when he sensed they were getting lazy. But more than act as an intermediate to the rich, he was grooming himself to be 'the rich man' one day. The poor man had himself to blame for his poverty.

India, the land of the Kamasutra, had become a very hypocritical conservative place. Adult movies and any skin show was restricted. But people were exploring their sexuality. No more was an adult movie a taboo. Multiple sexual partners were common. People were experimenting with Sex-droids.

Many English movie stars and Indians in western countries worked in the adult movie industry and made movies sold in India. There was a huge demand for local language and local environment adult movies that was not met with. He had met Kumb, and one discussion led to another and soon the lure of making some quick money made him finance an adult movie.

When he saw a young minor girl being brought to the set, he had stopped the pimp. He would not allow a minor girl in his movie and neither anyone be forced into it. It was business. Only those who wanted to make money using this route, could work for his financed venture. His conscience and speech motivated the staff. Kumb was impressed.

His demand that professional treatment be meted out to people working in his ventures had actually made people give their best ideas to him, and he rewarded them well. He was soon a known figure in the adult movie industry.

His biggest enemy would be piracy. Illegal copies of his illegal movies. He used his contacts with reputable distributors and found a clean good way of distributing these movies. He greased a lot of palms to ensure that no one copy his movies. His intimidating looks and harsh voice were good enough to send shivers down the worst of the bad guys. The pirates left his movies alone at least in the initial period.

Good decent people who did not want to get involved in this murky business, but wanted the quick returns financed him. He was very scrupulous with other people's money. He always gave each person their share and would rather give a rupee more than take one that was not his. His motto seemed to be, 'get rich and make others rich'.

His treatment of people and his high scruples brought him more financers. He was making very good money. Kumb was a highly talented director of adult movies. When he approached DM for turning his concept of a high-cost Mughal parody, DM had accepted. More because of Kumb's zeal and passion. At that time, he was not sure of the outcome.

But that turned out to be a huge success. The "Why be afraid when in Love" song was a huge success. The Prince and his lady-love making love with 100 young slaves dancing and making love around them in that exquisite set, with chandeliers and real diamonds in walls to reflect the light was downloaded 2.5 billion times. A record at that time.

Kumb followed this with episodes from the different lives of the Mughal kings and made parodies as in the west. He spent a fortune in recreating the Agra fort in an Island in the Indian ocean, the island controlled by DM's pirate friends. The series started from Akbar's harem and different sex parodies. By the time the parodies were completed, DM was already a multimillionaire. Three of the movies won the Adult movie awards. Kumb did the productions, under the banner of LKpati productions.

Following the success of his Red fort and Mughal king series, DM asked Kumb to take over many islands n the Indian Ocean. He recreated a Taj Mahal and made huge profits in his next series of sex in Taj Mahal.

Then Meghnath, another of their young upcoming officers in the organization had this sex tourism idea. He used the popularity of the Taj Mahal parody series and started a huge advertisement campaign in the LKpati Movies. Soon they were inundated with calls from rich couples who wanted to make love in the Taj Mahal like atmosphere. The entire costume, men and women (slaves in the Taj Mahal series movies) were rented out at exorbitant costs.

The Demand was so high that Meghnath had to build 300 Taj Mahals, each of the scale and detail of the original Taj Mahal. Tourists flocked to the Taj Mahal locations. The sets were rented on an hourly basis. People would play out the entire parody movie sequences. Full moon nights with all the colorful lights were the most popular occasions. The moolah DM raked was rumored to be more than the top three richest men in the universe put together.

With all this going on for him, DM wanted to enter the world of legitimacy. It is one thing to be feared and to be rich and another to be accepted by society as someone legitimate. People with old money looked down upon him. He wanted their acceptance.

He announced his grand enterprise of entering main stream cinema. However, the established players did not want him to go legitimate. They wanted him to keep making money for them, through his other ventures. Old money always looks with disdain at new money.

They did everything within their powers to stop him. It was a reputation and financial war like never before. DM pitted against the best in the universe. However, DM was determined to do what he wanted to do. Whatever they tried to use against DM; they found it being successfully deviated away from him. People would die for him rather than name him in any misdeed. They owned up DM's mistakes. They had become rich because of DM. They idolized him. The old money establishment realized that DM had grown more powerful than the old money establishment.

It was a two way war, and some of the old establishment's cronies were often trapped by DM's think tank. Soon there seemed to be a tilt in the balance. That is when the old establishment played it's trick. They felicitated DM and praised him. And in the felicitation, a concept-seed of DM trying a new starlet was put forward.

DM then announced that he would finance an extravagant 'Cinderella' story with fresh faces. He called in the best dress designers. The best sets were made, and talent search organized. It was a frenzy, like tinsel-town had never seen before.

And then he had seen Bhudevi. He informed that Bhudevi had to win the talent hunt. And so it happened.

In some way's the old establishment brought Bhudevi to his life. He had asked his directors and producers that the best costumes, sets and dialogues be made for Bhudevi. He showered praise upon her. He had servants available, and all Bhudevi had to do was move a finger, and everything that she desired would happen. She felt like a queen. She wanted delicate kathak dances in the movie as she was an expert in that. The script was re-written and Kathak dances introduced.

The script was changed a dozen times, taking the whims and fancies of Bhudevi's mind. The cine magazines had made a lot about the obvious attention DM was giving Bhudevi. The rumour mills were churning at top speed. Kumb paid the best critics and Magazines to cover the movie. The release was extravagant. Bhudevi lit the screen with her presence. It was a super hit.

DM felt that this was the correct time to approach Bhudevi with his proposal.

"Bhudeviji, Your performance was spectacular."

"Thank you sir."

"It is time you stopped calling me sir."

"Oh No sir! I can never do that."

"But you must. See these sets, these designers, the people around you. They all should belong to you. You are born to be a star. It is your destiny. I am ready to give all this to you."

"Oh thank you sir." Now wary of his advances.

"A princess lives differently. A princess has varied needs. She must be surrounded by the best of everything. See Bhudevi, only I have the wealth and reach to keep you where you belong. A princess among ordinary humans. Princesses should always live with Kings. We are destined to be together. Become my queen."

"Oh sir. I do not understand all this." Now feigning innocence, her discomfort visible.

"Bhudevi, I have been possessed by you. You have been in my mind taking my sleep away. You have stolen my heart. I wish to marry you."

"Oh no sir. I cannot."

"Don't say that. Don't feel intimidated by my wealth and power. Be mine, for all this is for you."

Bhudevi laughed. "No sir. I do not mean it that way. Only a girl who is very-very lucky can get all this. The reason I have to give this up is because I am in love with Raghav, and we plan to live together forever." Trying to sound as apologetic as possible.

DM was heartbroken. Raghav was the Son of a businessman. He had seen him a couple of times. A sharp business mind. someone who belonged to the old establishment.

The movie was a success. However, Bhudevi never worked for DM again, and her future ventures generally did 'OK'. Her career had its hits and misses. DM was heartbroken and entered into a kind of depression. It was rumored that his relationship with SharpNails or SN had brought him out of this depression. There were many ventures under the name SN corporation. Many people put DM and SN as one couple, but they were separate individuals.

DM instructed Kumb and Meghnath to start developing their subordinates, who could handle the smaller units. They would focus on business's worth billions.

Bhudevi soon moved in with Raghav, and they started their Live-in relationship.

A thousand women, many sex droids and so much of sex could not remove the image of Bhudevi from DM's mind. Every time he thought of her, he was turned on like an animal. Was it just lust? Was it fuelled by Bhudevi's rejection? He could never answer these questions.

CHAPTER 3

I looked at Suvi. One year gone and we still felt like it was day one. Suvi held my hand and did things under the blanket provided by the air hostess. Things she should not be doing in an aeroplane. The flight was short. We deplaned and took the airport express to Shivaji stadium metro station. And walked to our hotel in Connaught Place. Raghav was out of town, and this evening belonged to Suvi.

I wanted to take her to central park and Palika bazaar and do some 'bargain hunting'. However, we never got out of the bed.

We were both breathing heavily.

"So what do you think of this rape." She asked.

"Luckily I do not have to think of this rape."

"Have you read 'The rape of Lucrece'?"

"No. Luckily, we had more interesting subjects like electronics and programming to read in engineering."

"I think you should read. Rape is the ultimate physical assault on a woman's senses."

"Is there something in it for us?"

"What do you mean by that?"

"Is there some new technique described there?"

"You . . . . na . . . Think of something else once in a while." 'na' is an expression that appears in Indian English. It generally seeks acknowledgement or as in this case stresses on the subject.

"Why? Won't there be an old age happening for that. Some forty or fifty years down the line?" I had seen some ads for the new drug for older men. They could do it three to four times a week at 90 years. We were like doing it six to seven times a day. I hoped that by the time we were old, the drugs could let us keep this frequency. Or do we get tired of all this by that time. I hoped not.

"With you! I think it is never going to come." She meant that old age. I hoped that it would never come.

"Or you wish it would never come."

"Now stop it. Don't touch here, my nipples are hurting. Enough for one day." After a pause, "I am serious. You must read this work."

"Ok what's in it?"

"Just read it."

So I Google'd 'The rape of Lucrece'. There is the Openshakesphere website, and I read the poem, but the language was very old English. I read the synopsis. It looked like a nobleman had raped a noble lady, and the deed's atrocity brought the king to his exile, and a republic was established.

"Did you like it?"

I did not want Suvi to start a discussion on the poem. She should have been a professor who analyzed the written word to detail. She admonished me on my English quite regularly, and I quipped that the days when you had to follow the language's syntax and semantics of a far away island in Europe was over. The English language was evolving and the way we talked, was getting added to the dictionary, thesaurus and grammar of the language.

I noted that like Hindi movies, the woman committed suicide. The poet had not described anything that could add to my knowledge of techniques.

"The woman commits suicide and they take revenge. I wonder if that used to be the norm in those days."

"Yes. In those days, a woman who had sex outside of her marriage was supposed to be impure. Even if she was raped."

"So if the male protruding object were to go into the impure recessed female object, then the Male object was not supposed to have gotten impure! Ha Ha." When we engineers want to be politically correct we use such language.

She did not share my sense of humour. She thought that I was being crass and vulgar, while I felt that I had technically described something instead of using the actual words for the organs as described in the English language by the P and V words or the act as described in most street language by the F word.

"You are impossible!"

But I pressed the protruding object a little more. Let her know where I was. She giggled and gave in.

"Let's have dinner at Nirula's."

"What is this chain?"

"It was a hyped western chain when it was established, and the fusion food was supposed to be the order of the day. However, they did not grow outside of Delhi. You can still get a good 'big brother burger' and Hot chocolate fudge, which is cold."

"OK. We can try that tonight."

Getting her to Nirula's was also a way to get her to go with me to Palika Bazaar and to walk through central park in Delhi. I had seen this revealing maid's costume in one of the store's online catalogue. It would be fun to buy it from a shop. Try to bargain with the salesman or droid there. I knew the routines. As soon as I turned up, the droid would scan my retina and identify me. And my likes and dislikes, previous purchase history and my wish lists would pop up in the Droid's memory. The salesman would see it on the computer screen kept generally below the counter top, so that we could not see all this.

Instantly, it would show him the items that I would have a high probability of buying. Get my favorite color's and things like that. I had done some of that programming. There was also a random algorithm. Generally, after three items from history, the droid had to try to sell me the popular items or choose a random item. Would the droid guess what I had in mind? That would be something to experience.

We walked to the Nirula's in Connaught street. I had the big brother burger combo with the soup and the hot chocolate fudge. Suvi was satisfied with a simple Pizza.

On our way back, I took her to Palika Bazar. We scanned some Indian ethnic Salvar Kameez ladies outfits. Suvi was surprised at the low prices there. And she was surprised when I bargained after the guys quoted those low prices.

She brought herself some retro Punjabi salvaar and kameez that were coming back in fashion. And it would be a new fashion in Mumbai.

I took her to the store I was interested in. She had the same mischievous smile that I had anticipated she would. The cyber droid probably found that I had purchased sixteen baby-dolls night wear in the last year and started showing me some of that. So the purchasing logic was still in vogue. Then suddenly it guessed the maid party dress that I had in mind! I wondered how the program had sensed this.

Then I saw the hidden camera's in various locations in the shop. All retina movements were being captured. And the change in retinal opening or whatever changes in eye's, as soon as you saw something of interest was captured as a probable target! Things had changed.

I should see some of the code in my head. I then followed the cues from the sales droid. There was a male front opening underwear that he offered and a few other things. So I got some stuff which I guessed were in Suvi's mind. We had interesting few days ahead of us!

"Good collection. Na . . ."

I looked up and saw two intimidating types in the shop. Our exit from the shop was blocked.

"Yes. You may shop now." I tried to be pleasant and tried to make a way between them, signaling with my hand.

"You look new here. You should be careful in new places. Don't poke your nose where it does not belong." He tried to give me a 'You get me' kind of look in a threatening way.

"You must have got me mixed with someone else." I was smiling trying to put my pleasantest smile. I could be rough. I had done my self defense courses and also learnt some martial arts. I visited the gym regularly and stayed fit.

They made way for me to go. I held Suvi's hand, and we went past them.

"We are watching you." One of them said.

To get threatened even before the case could start was something new.

CHAPTER 4

I walked into Raghav's office. I was surprised at the move to have an in-person meeting with Raghav. Nowadays, most of the Meetings are done via 3D holographic imaging. The next generation of devices were ones where the device would send messages directly to the brain and get the reactions and responses in microseconds.

A book of a thousand pages could be read in one microsecond. The knowledge and interaction like the Bhagwat Gita between Lord Krishna and Arjun or the Ashtavakra gita between Sage Ashtavakra and King Janak could happen in less than a microsecond.

However, these were banned and even research on this had been halted. People were afraid that this would make some maniac control people's thoughts and actions. Turn them into slaves and stuff like that. Paranoia!

Raghav looked tense, maybe a bit worried. This was not the Raghav, I had seen when he was helping Sugriv. He was always beaming. Full of confidence, even when all looked lost. He motioned me to sit across the table. The office had comfortable couches.

"Tea, Coffee?"

"Herbal tea." I have been told that all this tea coffee, alcohol and cigarettes affect your libido and so keep away from these. People attribute this to some saintly quality in me or to various gods that we believe in or consider me a 'good human being'. I welcome all these side benefits!

He touched a button and ordered two herbal teas.

"Was the journey comfortable?"

"Yes."

"Sugriv told me that you had a vacation planned, and I dragged you into this."

"It is destiny."

Bhudevi arrived with the Tea. I was surprised to see a beaming Bhudevi. She did not look like someone in post abduction or rape trauma. I had seen her a couple of times. She is quite a looker. Her beauty is not the demure, girlish kind of look, but she has a bit of naughtiness on her face. She reminds me of a classic heroine in a movie "Tanu weds Manu". She should have tried some vamp roles. I was sure that she would be a hit as a 'vamp with a heart' kind of role. However, she was the old money billionaire Raghav's wife. No one probably dared to suggest it. She had to be the heroine, and she had to be in a clean character in every movie.

She served tea and left. I was uncomfortable broaching the subject of Rape with Raghav. If you think of it, how do you say, 'tell me the details of the rape of your wife?' I am too much of a straight shooter, but this was something I was not groomed for. I sipped my tea and said:

"How can we ask her about the 'Incident'?" I stressed on incident. I did not want Raghav to be uncomfortable.

Raghav laughed for the first time.

"Oh Anjani! She is not Bhudevi. She is just a droid. Bhu (Bhudevi) has to travel quite frequently because of her work. I cannot bear to be without her." I could understand that. I hated being away from Suvi even for a day.

"So I asked our Droid divisions to create several droids of Bhu. I think I should congratulate them. They have done a wonderful work."

"Yes Sir. I could not believe that she was not human." The skin would be made from exotic silicon-elastomer materials. Totally non toxic. I had heard that the rich could make droids with so many features. Model them on any popular person. The skin is made from recultivated dead cells multiplied using some stem cell technology. A perfect companion. Most companies in this business focused on the sexual aspects, but some focused on companionship, knowledge and secretarial skills. I could obviously not ask what type of Bhudevi like droids Raghav had.

"Yes the skin, the fragrance, the voice, memories and everything are exactly like Bhudevi's. It is the next-best thing to having Bhu next to me." A sadness creeping into his voice.

I felt sympathy towards this great person. He was brought up in a family with a golden spoon to his mouth. He at some point decided to give his wealth and control of family business to his younger brother. Then started on his own, struggled to make it big and later built an empire on his own. And what a younger brother to have. He had always said that he was only playing proxy to Raghav and awaited the day when Raghav had fulfilled his desire to create an empire and would hand it over to Raghav. Examples of kinship that is missing in these days.

Raghav had terra forming businesses in Mars, Titan and three other celestial bodies. The old businesses of insurance, automobiles, aircraft and what not being effectively run by his younger brother. He also had some forays into the Droid business. However, his company focused more on companion droids.

"Then how can we talk to Bhudeviji and get started?"

"Let me begin the story from the start.

We got married soon after her first movie. Initially, I traveled with her to various locations, and we were inseparable. The family business had different needs, so I handed the reins to my brother as per my father's wishes or rather against his. I also wanted to do something on my own. Bhudevi and I struggled for some time."

Yes there had been a time, when Raghav had millions and not the billions that he was used to. That would seem like abject poverty to Raghav.

"Then my businesses also started to grow. Bhudevi started accepting offers where she had to shoot in the same town as I was. However, there were song sequences in movies and some stuff that needed her to travel. Then I asked my Droid division to make the first droid. And the droid made had to be so good that the droid could travel in place of Bhudevi, and Bhudevi could be with me. In almost 12 movies, the droid was used. It was almost impossible, except for the most discerning eye and those knowing Bhudevi closely to find out where the droid is used."

This was news to me. Droid seconds were being used in many difficult to perform action scenes. That much was known. Use for regular scenes was not known. Droid movements were not as fluid as human beings.

"I wanted to start my own production house, but Bhu was always against it. She kept saying that if it was an in-house production, then she could never know if she was good or not. She would always be in the lead role, and that would ruin her efforts to keep her acting up to the mark. Being the owner's wife, we would be surrounded by sycophants rather than genuine artists.

She wanted to do some roles that needed her to explore the other planets. Since we had businesses almost everywhere, this was easy to accommodate. However, our separations grew. Knowing how much I missed her, she asked our droid staff to make a next-generation droid. A droid with which we could do everything that we did with each other." Finally getting to the point on the purpose of the droids.

"But Anjani, do not misunderstand us. We do not believe in sex droids like others. This was to be our conduit to each other. Whatever Bhudevi wanted to say to me, she could say to my droid with her, and Bhu's droid would say to me. It was like being with each other. We did not want programs and libraries of information to answer each other.

It was not like we were living with a droid because the droids every external cell was programmed to do exactly what we as persons were doing. Do you get me?"

"Somewhat. You guys did not want a 100% droid. You used the droid to only do what the other person was doing." I tried to simplify the actions.

"Yes. Of course, we used the droids only when we were free from our activities and in our free time."

"Yes I understand that. I was using an old chat program and in ancient times people would chat by coming near a computer."

"Yes you got the point. Except that instead of the computer, we were in front of the droid.

Then we started exploring other possibilities of intimacy. This usage of droids was known only to the two of us."

He paused.

"Then last year, she was contacted by an old film maker to work in an ancient work. Shakuntala. The entire shooing was to happen in Mars. We have several terra forming projects there. And so she could stay in our large guest house in Tholus." There was a small town named Tholus in Mars now. A Crème-de-la-Crème place.

"Since the separation was prolonged . . . . I was tied up in some business here. And she was too busy in doing the movie. We started using the droids for more intimate activities. Then of late, I started getting more requests for sex. Bhu doing things that she would never do in real life with me. I got suspicious. I asked her some questions, the answers to which only Bhu knew. However, she avoided or could not answer, and mysteriously our communication systems would break down.

Day before yesterday, I sent my partner in Mars; his name is Lucky, to check on Bhu. He informed me that he had met Bhu. However, the Bhu in Tholus was a droid. He tried to split open the Droid. However, the droid disintegrated destroying all the data, the tapes, the disks and everything. Bhu had disappeared without a trace."

"So this is not a rape but a kidnapping."

"Yes and No. Why would someone kidnap Bhu? Money could be one motive. However, to make the ruined droid would have cost the person a fortune. Believe me, we will see this ruined droid. Everything was similar or better than the droid that our company had made. The materials used were most advanced. Everything, skin, body odor everything was same as Bhudevi. Somebody has spent a fortune to make this droid. The droid was learning from me to have another possible Raghav droid behave the same way with Bhu.

I believe this could be some crazed rich fan. Someone with millions to spend on his lust for a woman. There is no ransom request. That is why I suspect that this has a sexual angle. So I sent for you."

There was no point in wasting time on frivolities.

"Let's see this droid."

Raghav and I walked to another room. A scientist in an apron was examining a droid. The face was badly damaged. Almost human like. Some of the head was burnt and damaged, exposing a skull inside.

"Hi Sachchit. This is Anjani. A very dear friend. He has come to help us trace Bhudevi. And Anjani, this is

Sachchit. Chief scientist at our droid works. He was responsible for creating our Bhudevi droid."

I knew Sachchit or rather had heard about him. The creator of the first modern droid. He had made the first companion droid for Raghav's corporate. The concept was entirely new at that time. People had never seen anything like this before. He was a legend among technocrats.

"Well Anjani, let me cut short the chase. This Droid has the same skull material as we do. Made from a special process of making a mold using actual human and animal bones along with a bonding silico elastomer. I suspect some stem cells have been used in making parts of the Droid. This gives it almost the same weight as a human skull of the same dimension. The skull and skeleton and all bones are almost an exact replica of Bhudeviji's bone structure. So they had access to the entire skeletal structure of Bhudevi. Of course, the droid moves using different mechanics. So to that extent the bone structure differs.

The external skin is made from a cultured human skin and just beneath is a layer made with a special kind of silico-elastomer compound. In fact the material is better than the one we use. We get a 0.5mm X 0.5mm square cell size. Oh Sorry, let me explain.

The skin of human beings is made of pores, epidermis and muscles etc. When we make a droid, the skins features like color, odor, perspiration rate, its expansion or contraction is done by injecting nano electrical signals into a lattice of silico-elastomer. This electric signal changes the property for a certain area of the skin, releases some stored odor. In our case, we have a 0.5mm X 0.5mm or 0.25sq mm area that is individually controlled.

The sex droid business is really a booming business. We make companion Droids. We sell anywhere between 1-2 million droids each year. We make some sex droids, just to be in the industry. The real leader is SN droids." Sachchit obviously wanted to enter the Sex droid business at a faster pace, and someone in the organization was holding him back. Finally, they had to consider their companion droid business's reputation.

"Any ways, Sex droids could be selling 200 times that number. People model them after the girls or women they fancy, the men I mean. And women and girls on boys and men they fancy, super stars, cine stars, singers, sports persons you name it. An average individual buys 3-4 droids a year. The ticket size is a few thousand dollars per droid for the mass-produced ones. And every individual buys one that costs upwards of 50 thousand dollars, once a few years. Now though this may seem a small ticket size per individual, companies spend billions on research for the next thing in droids. A large part is celebrity endorsements and studies. Celebrities body odor, features, common expressions are studied and then incorporated into the droids. A new model may start at 15-20 thousand dollars and then gradually reduce within a few weeks after release.

Then the droid pirate companies will start making cheap copies. The price drops down to 3-4 thousand dollars. And once the market is saturated; we go for the next model.

The average cell size of the common droids is 2mm X 2 mm and for the good ones around 1mm X 1 mm. The controls are more rudimentary. However, so are human beings. If your cheeks grow red, an area of 20mm X 20mm could go red. So even a 2mm X2mm is pretty accurate. The technology difference between the original models and cheaper pirated models are pretty thin.

This droid has a 0.1 X 0.1 cell size. In short, it is 25 times more accurate than us in terms of expressions, odor, color change or expansion/contraction or stiffness changes. The computer has to work 25 times faster and is an advanced microchip.

And the most advanced droids like the one we made of Bhudevi and this one have skin grafted from regenerated dead cells of the human being. This sits on top of the silico-elastomer and has some enzymes and glands below that keep the skin alive and makes it respond like a live human person. The silico-elastomer becomes a kind of epidermis.

The most amazing or scary thing is that the skin has the same composition as Bhudevi's. Almost as if someone had access to Bhudevi like we did."

"How much would it have cost to make this cyber droid?" Raghav wanted to know.

"My rough estimate based on our experience is around 25 million. Give or take a few millions. This being the first one, a lot of research has to go into it."

"So the person who has done this is rich. How many companies have his kind of resource?"

"Frankly sir, there are quite a few billionaires. However, only thirty or forty who would go to this extent. If it is an individual, then the numbers are small. However, if there is an organization behind this venture that wants to blackmail or use or study Bhudeviji to make the next droid based on her, then the number of probable's rises multifold. There is a huge demand for Bhudeviji. She is one of the few celebrities today who has not signed up with any droid company. Her body is a total mystery. And we constantly track any pirate company that claims or fakes a Bhudevi droid. She has more than fifty million fans. If any Droid on her is released, then it would sell by tens of millions in the first few days."

"I do not think it is any organization that wants to release a Bhudevi droid. See any organization that does this, has to release the droid in the market. The moment they do that, they would be facing a litigation. No company would dare to do this."

"Not in the open. However, there are some companies that do specialize in releasing data to a close circle. With each such droid costing around 5 million or so."

"So there is no company that would invest a quarter billion in making a droid first, then kidnapping Bhudevi. What purpose does that serve? They already have the droid. They do not need Bhudevi. This is something more sinister. There is somebody who is super rich and is crazed about her. We need to find out who it is."

Raghav's analysis seemed to make sense.

"I would like to start with knowing what programming and memory information we have. Every chip, every component that has been used, has to come from somewhere. So we start from that point.

I want every component and its sources.

Every elastomer or silico-elastomer manufacturer and research agency doing high end research, anyone who could be capable of making this.

And let us not forget the movie that Bhudevi was supposed to work in. I want all the details of that movie company.

I want all the details of program lines and codes that can be deciphered from the chips and memory devices inside.

I will give a list of agencies who are good at this kind of work.

I have to make a call to Sugriv to arrange for these guys to be available."

"Good thinking Anjani." There was some rekindling of hope in Raghav. He probably felt that he had chosen the right person for the job.

Raghav further added "I had said that I was out on business yesterday. However, I was in Tholus. Doing some investigation there." Raghav had a ½ light speed nuclear powered space craft. It would have taken him roughly an hour to reach Tholus from earth. "We have a Droid unit there. Bhu used to leave with the droid pilots and fly to the shooting site. It is an exquisite set. Gigantic artificial trees and what not. And she would return every evening. The makeup van was supposed to be from the movie company. We practically do not know when the switch happened. It should have been five or six days ago. The Movie van there has nothing in it. There is no one on site. My unit is doing a DNA analysis of the location and sets. So far, no trace. Looks like everyone there was a droid. I will handover the report to you. The Movie unit is a new registered unit. The set was rented. The names and all addresses are false. No trace anywhere. The whole setup was very well financed. All this is included in the report." Raghav turned on a monitor that was connected to Lucky in Tholus.

"Nothing Raghav. Look at this van." We saw a holographic image of the Van. He opened the door, and he walked in. The 3D hologram camera also walked in. There was some distortion. "There is hardly anything in here. Looks like someone switched the entire van."

"They seem to be aware of all your moves." I added.

"Why do you say that?" I informed Raghav about the incident with the two goons at Palika bazaar the last evening.

"Hmnnn . . . we will check and weed out any leaks in our organization. However, of your arrival, only Sugriv and myself knew. I had sent an email from my Droid station."

"Sachchit, can you bring this droid station. I will check it with some tools."

As expected the Droid station had an outdated firewall and some outdated antivirus—anti spyware.

As they say, "The blame lies within ourselves!"

CHAPTER 5

The council of the world.

That is what they called themselves. It had been in existence since pre-historic times. Their actions were called as actions by the gods then. They controlled the world from time immemorial. They decided the course of humanity. Membership was by invitation only, and it was not passed from father to child. Even close family members were not supposed to be informed of their membership to the council. Their word was more than the law. They had resources beyond ordinary politicians and individual's comprehension. They wielded power to change kings and Queens.

They watched DM grow. Initially, from a distance and then as his business size grew, with more interest. They watched DM and his organization very closely. Some were wary of the clout that this organization was gathering. DM was becoming too powerful. They could not trounce him or his businesses. Their first attempt to thwart him to a small size was when he had wanted to enter the Movie business, and had failed.

When it failed, they realized that he was becoming more powerful than the old establishment of businessmen. Either he had to be a part of the council or his size had to be cut down. There had been many tainted members in the past. Including DM in the council would not be difficult. There were many old money people in the council and they may object.

Post the incident with his legitimate movie business, they tried to thwart him from entering the droid business and later the terra forming business. However, DM was very deft at maneuvering his organization towards its goals.

The concern among the council members was growing. Now they had more people watching DM's every move. For the first time, the council had to expand in size, roping in more people from the old establishment. Increase in size of the council body had huge risks. The possibility of a slip or leak increased many fold with the induction of each new member.

It's current chairman was an American, and his name for council activities was "Wish Washington." Wish had taken over after the last failure from the council to thwart DM's terraforming project.

Wish had promised to cut down DM's clout. There were many possibilities, DM could incur a huge financial loss, tailored by the council. However, DM would also have to make some bad moves or investments that would lose. That seemed improbable. DM had a good business sense.

The second option was to get DM involved in some personal thing in life, making him divert his energy to some lady or affair or something that could keep his mind tied up. Wish got his dossier on DM and DM's closest. He zoomed in onto the head of DM's droid business. SharpNails!

SharpNails was one of the modern lot. Sleeping with a new male almost every night. She was independent. And she made droids of the most interesting men in the world for herself. Her palatial home in an Island was supposed to have 2000 Droids and men at her beck and call. She was living her every dream.

So the first angle of blackmail would not work with her. She would openly accept her acts. And in addition, she was utterly devoted to DM. There was no way she could be turned in to help them against DM. She would lay her life to save DM.

SharpNails approached Raghav during a chance meeting at a droid summit. She made many overtures towards Raghav. However, Raghav smoothly turned them down and kept the discussions businesslike. SharpNails was also caught in a security camera footage, placing her hand over Rahghav's thighs. A bold sexual move. However, Raghav had taken her hand away and moved to another part of the room. Wish was one of the few who had access to such videos. This seemed like an interesting angle to explore.

And Wish had read the dossier on DM, again and again. There were so many rumors that DM was interested in Bhudevi, before her marriage. There seemed to be an angle to exploit. Wish knew that SharpNails had secretly built a few Bhudevi like droids for DM. She had also built a few Raghav like droids for herself.

Wish hit upon a plan. It had its loose ends, but sometimes, it is the stretched imagination that works. During a summit on Droids, he planted his trusted aide, Nadir in a key position. As anticipated, SharpNails could not resist the charming young Nadir. She made the necessary overtures. Nadir responded positively. By that evening, there were in SharpNails Island.

"You seem to be infatuated by Raghav."

"No these are just collections."

"A Raghav slave droid that you whip, a Raghav droid with a large tongue for obvious reasons, a Raghav droid as a pilot. Aw c'mon! You can tell papa."

"It was just that he is handsome in many ways."

"He is a shrewd businessman and some toned body, but he and his wife are so stiff. I think they are frigid. I wanted a Bhudevi droid and couldn't get one. They are so chaste with each other that I almost hate them for that. There is some suspense created due to that, but as they grow older, it seems just like . . . hmnnn . . . wasted youth."

"I can make a Bhudevi droid for you. It is expensive, but most of her details are well captured."

"You mean you used some hidden cameras for getting her body details."

"Some were from hidden camera's. Some from computer analysis. But Raghav and Bhudevi's sex routines are their secrets. We have only made algorithmic guesses. Based on their star sign, social upbringing and things like that."

"That's not the real thing."

"It is the best that is available."

"Unless someday they offer their secrets to the public."

"I do not think that is happening soon."

"Now think if Bhudevi were to go to a movie shoot. In Tholus maybe. And Raghav is here. A droid replaces Bhudevi. While the actual Bhudevi is analyzed and made to cooperate."

"Such criminal thoughts!" SharpNails was surprised at this suggestion from Nadir. She had never thought of doing something like this to get Bhudevi to cooperate.

"It is wishful thinking. However, from time immemorial, people have been satisfying their lust for the high and mighty in any way possible. I read an ancient text named "The Fan Club" and they kidnap a heroine and have sex with her. However, as you say, it is never going to happen with the likes of Raghav and Bhudevi."

"But still Plausible." She must read this book; she thought.

"Why are we discussing such imbeciles, who are not interested in our way of life."

And then the council planted the seed of a Movie in Bhudevi's mind during a cocktail party. The council used Mark to lay the idea of Shakuntala and how the movie would turn the fortunes of Bhudevi. The set would be Near Tholus. The permission to use one of Kumb's studio's near Tholus was anonymously made and removed.

Now to keep Raghav busy and hope for the best.

Everything had worked as they had hoped for. They had set the stage, and things had fallen in place.

Now to point Raghav in the right direction and "CheckMate."

Nadir knocked and entered Wish's office. He gave a thumbs-up.

"Our people hired two goons to threaten Anjani."
"Good. That should drive him hard into the chase."
"Now for phase-2 of the plan."

SharpNails, well that is what she said was the translation of her Chinese name, was born lower middle class but had a fierce ambition. She would have done anything to succeed. And she was as much a nymphomaniac as she was ambitious. She considered herself a tigress or a rare kind of Cleopatra, who enslaved men. Her ambition to grow really fast led her to DM's organization. She had started low in the Droid organization that Meghnath had started. It lacked a total sense of direction. They were there because they were there. They did not love the droids. They did not want to create the best!

Now SharpNails was a rare kind of woman, who was driven by sex. Every aspect of her life had to have some sex in it. She loved to talk sex and watch sex and be in an environment where sex dominated everything. She was so passionate about incorporating the best in the droids. She studied older items like vacuum pumps, dildo's, eggs, You cups, Tenga and what not. She had every detail of every sex tool ever made in her mind. Her passion to excel did not go unnoticed.

It was Meghnath who saw her potential and moved her to the helm, reserving a role as an advisor to the board. A rare gesture, where a chief of an organization realizes that a subordinate is better than them in their line of business.

SharpNails had a lot of ideas and wanted to take this Droid business to the next level. She needed a lot of budget, and since it would be something new that they would be doing, it involved a lot of risk. She wanted to approach DM, But DM was known to be in a sulky mood. The top level knew that he was hurting from Bhudevi's rejection. He was trying to focus on business and growth but finding it difficult to achieve. He could be irritable, and though he did not sack anyone in that mood or during that phase of his life, people around him were more wary.

SharpNails pitched to DM, urging him to support her plans for expanding the R&D on droids. Sex droid business was booming, but people were still selling silicon dolls with vibrators and some bare skeleton. She combined her degree in Robotics and in human anatomy to create some fusion droids. DM was not impressed at first. Even with the silly dolls and vibrations, sales were so high, that they need not innovate.

So SharpNails and her team buried in work in their lab and came out with the first prototype. It was a 5X5 mm cell size Bhudevi droid, with some metallic skeleton. The private parts were rudimentary. Sound and dialogues were taken from Bhudevi's first movie. SharpNails was confident that some of the dialogues in the movie were DM's brainchild.

SharpNails made a bold move and took the Bhudevi droid to DM's home. When DM entered his house, he was surprised to find Bhudevi sitting on a couch in a dimly lit area.

She welcomed him with "I have been waiting for you to come to me Nath." Nath meaning lord!

A corny dialogue that DM inserted in the movie, and specifically imagining Bhudevi saying the same to him.

"Hi Bhudeviji."

"Hi DM."

He switched on the light. This was not Bhudevi, but a droid. His phone rang. It was that Chinese girl.

"Surprised." She asked.

DM did not like the ruse and muttered "Hmmm."

"I'm sorry to have poked my nose into your personal business. Just give me the budget, and I will create a Bhudevi, who will be exactly the Bhudevi of this world. Every word, every syllable will be like from Bhudevi. Thought process, smell, softness of skin and everything else will be exact. I will make a Bhudevi for you who will be utterly more beautiful than the actual Bhudevi. Something that Raghav will never be able to have!

Again, my apologies for entering into your personal life, but I could not bear seeing you sad."

That personal touch and someone understanding his mental tussle with Raghav, registered in DM's mind. So DM invited SharpNails to his home. SharpNails was intrigued by DM's passion for Bhudevi and also felt a little jealous. She touched DM's shoulder. DM needed some love and compassion. Their sex was quite explosive.

A few days with SharpNails, and DM returned to his senses. He was focusing on business and on other women. The sulkiness was gone. SharpNails felt her womanhood vindicated. She may not be able to replace Bhudevi in DM's life, but she had got him over it.

She broached the subject of the Droids with DM. The Droids needed to become more realistic, more human.

"There are many like you who faced the dilemma, when women turn fickle or get sidetracked by other men or women, need some solace and such droids can provide it."

DM had seen some value in what she had said, and she got her budget.

SharpNails was actually the one who gave a future direction to this industry. The first thing she did was clear the budget for R&D on Silico-elastomers.

The real brains behind the droids were the controls and speech controls. The companion droid needed to be a good conversationalist. The book lovers droid had to be a library of books that the droid would read, then there were nanny droids, and many other types.

However, the largest sellers were the sex droids.

All needed separate algorithms and devices to control the droids. The controls' budget was the highest ever.

With this high control's budget, she ensured that the right amount of database of words and expressions were included. The droids could now carry out intelligent conversations. However, the voice was clipped and sounded mechanical.

SharpNails realized that it is not the perfections that make us human, but rather our imperfections. That drawl in speech, the minor mispronunciations and phonetic errors define our speech.

The next phase of investment was where these imperfections were built in. It required more effort than making perfect robots. During this phase, a person's individual speech style, the drawls, the little imperfections were analyzed and programmed and more importantly, new algorithms for these imperfections evolved. With this innovation, the droids became more human like.

She also increased the motor control division and grafting and stem cell division budgets. The siloco-elastomer size was reduced to 1mmX1mm size in all commercial droids. Their Droids suddenly ruled the markets. The then market leader in droids, Raghav's enterprise was reduced to number two.

DM was overjoyed. He felt very close to SharpNails. He named many of the enterprises in the droid business after SharpNails or SN corporation.

SharpNails also made droids with better resolution for special orders. Like the one for DM.

Once the innovation juggernaut gained momentum, they discovered a method of multiplying skin cells from dead skins using some of the stem cell technologies. The skin could be kept alive using a special blood like fluid that filled a few microns of space between the silico-elastomer exterior and the skin. The skin had to be thin enough to pass on the changes on the siico-elastomer to the external appearance.

This required more controls and a finer integration of the silico-elastomer and external skin.

The droid's mannerisms, skin tone, odor and everything matched that of the human being who was getting droidized.

Her teams were reducing silico-elastomer cell sizes by some microns every day. The controls were also becoming more accurate and complex.

With the exteriors going through this revolution, for some time the internals were neglected. The same-old dildo technology dominated male organs, and the cylinders and cups made room in the women's organs.

SharpNails asked her teams to make exact human-like organs. She drove her personnel to work hard and motivated them to be perfectionists. For this, they used stem cell research to grow male and female organs in an external environment. These organs had to be sustained in a silico-elastomer base frame with artificial fluids. The organs should have exact changes in unexcited, excited and peak arousal states.

At every incremental stage of development, she personally tested each organ. Suggested improvisations and added enhancements. A male organ was no longer limited to a metallic, plastic or glass dildo but the organ was an exact male organ with additions like thousands of tongues that came out once inside the female human organ space and did wonders. The female organ had similar such enhancements and a small vacuum pump that maintained a slight negative pressure. She had created droids that were the talk of the town. Once people started using these advanced droids, they found sex with another human quite boring.

SharpNails now had the exact technology and advancements for Droids and rival organizations like those of Ragav's could not imagine in their dreams.

As the technology progressed, she kept replacing the Bhudevi droids for DM. With each new development and new Bhudevi droid, DM's excitement in this technology grew.

She plotted new ways to increase DM's experience. DM was at one hand the person who had made all this possible for her and on the other, he was a measure of how much joy and satisfaction her technology could bring to others. She saw DM totally devoting his free time to his Bhudevi Droids. Doing things for the droid and talking with the droid and making homes for the Bhudevi droid that were artistic marvels. She could see the depth of DM's feeling for Bhudevi from these acts.

What a stupid girl Bhudevi turned out to be! Abandoning all this for that childish Raghav. SharpNails had Bhudevi invited to many of her parties or arranged parties where she would be present. Invariably, Raghav would appear. Initially, she studied their mannerisms and had a secret team make speech and mannerism wise exact replicas of Raghav and Bhudevi.

Once she invited Bhudevi to a new movie launch party and made Raghav the chief guest. She had the whole evening planned to perfection. Both Raghav and Bhudevi were given a pedicure and manicure, and all their dead cells collected. Whatever they touched was unannounced whisked away. So many samples were collected. Both were also secretly x rayed.

Within days, she made skins for the next version of Raghav and Bhudevi Droids for DM and herself. DM could not express his pleasure, when he came to know the extent, SharpNails had gone to create the Bhudevi droid.

Though externally she had everything of Bhudevi made to perfection, she knew that these were not 100% the same. There was conjecture where they had placed Bhudevi's internal organs, the shapes and sizes of internal organs were also a conjecture. How Bhudevi's droid behaved in bed was also a best guess. It was like they Were this close, but it was not the 'exact' stuff.

With DM's fiftieth approaching, she wanted to surprise him. Give him something that would blow away his mind.

And it was in this background that she met Nadir in that fateful party.

That simple conversation with him laid the seed for making an audacious plan.

It was in her party that Mark had discussed the movie "Shakuntala" with Bhudevi. SharpNails had been quite near Mark and Bhudevi, within hearing distance and heard everything.

'Why is he wasting his time on her. She is not available to anyone other than Raghav.'

However, the seeds germinated in her mind, and she created a most audacious plan.

For the plan to succeed, she needed the assistance of Kumb and Megnath. DM had to be convinced.

"Look DM, we all know . . . this infatuation that Bhudevi has for Raghav is a mirage. She has not felt real love. She does not understand your passion.

What does she know of life and love other than what Raghav has offered? Nothing! She has not experienced lovemaking with a real man. Someone with your experience.

Once we have isolated her from Raghav and provided her with sexual experiences with our droids, then she cannot refuse your love.

She will gladly forget Raghav and be yours forever."

"I do not want to cause her any hurt."

'No, you will not. Rather, you will make her realize her true love. She will understand that there is nothing in that child Raghav. Opportunity has to be created to make her understand what she deserves.

It would be your own fault that you have not made your true love realize her potential"

And so DM was won by her arguments.

Kumb arranged for a young producer to float a proxy company.

It could not be traced to them. Meghnath had made the set for "Shakuntala—the movie." Bhudevi was signed along with a large cast.

The shooting started with Bhudevi coming every day from Tholus.

SharpNails made all the arrangements. The makeup van had many secret cameras. And that was how she had seen the Raghav droid.

The snatching of Bhudevi was very simple. One day, a sweet-smelling gas emanated from the air conditioner in the van, and Bhudevi was rendered unconscious. The van was replaced, and a Bhudevi droid started going to Tholus.

Bhudevi woke up and found herself in a room with a big TV. There seemed to be no doors or the doors were seamlessly built into the room. She could see some external light seeping in through what looked like a sliding partition. As she walked towards it, it opened automatically, revealing a garden. She did not venture out. She was feeling drowsy and tired, and so she lay and fell asleep again. When she woke up, she wondered what she was doing in this strange place.

Had she fallen unconscious?

Had she slept off in the set?

It took her some time to question the possibility that she had been abducted.

DM approached her, and she was nervous.

"Hi."

"What is the meaning of all this?"

"Bhudevi, do not get angry. I have arranged for you to be here so that we can be together. You need to understand my love and give it a chance. This seemed the only way. So I took my chances."

"Are you out of your mind! You have kidnapped me and brought me here."

"Why are you using such harsh words? You know my love for you. I want you to see my love. That is all. You are here, and that is the truth. Make the best of it."

"Are you out of your mind! I am eternally tied to Raghav. He is my husband. I cannot belong to anyone else. You can keep me anywhere for ages, and still I will belong top Raghav."

"He is not your husband. You two never married. You have a live in relationship."

"Marriage is not a legal certificate. We are committed to each other, and that is our marriage certificate. However, I need not be explaining this to you. Just let me go."

"You are here because it is your destiny. You have no choice but to be mine. You want to go, well you are free to go. But where will you go? There is nowhere to go."

"It is by your evil design that I am here and not because of my destiny. When Raghav comes to know of my disappearance, he will move heaven and earth to get me back."

"Ha ha ha. What will he do? At this point, he is talking with the droid that is in your place. And if he does come to know that you have disappeared, then he will chase that movie company. He will never know where you are. I can have him smashed in a day, but my philosophy is live and let live. Soon a beautiful girl will enter his life, and you will be forgotten."

"Never!"

"Just watch it happen. Everything will be recorded and shown to you. You will realize how fickle your love was. What a wrong choice you have made in life. Had it not been for me, your life and love would have been wasted. You will see, and you will be mine soon. I have full faith in this. Just relax and enjoy your stay here. This is no longer your or my destiny. It is our destiny."

Bhudevi felt desperate. She did not have any means of sending information out. Every hour seemed to prolong into endless time. She kept her resolve by remembering Raghav's face. How stupid of her to have forced Raghav to let her do this movie.

She was sure that Raghav would not be interested in any other woman. DM was demented, but Raghav was sane.

He would find a way to get to her. He would get her out.

Where was she?

Somewhere in Mars or was she in another planet or satellite?

She had no idea.

Panic seized her for a moment. What if Raghav was never able to trace her location?

No he will find me.

He has to.

He loves me.

Will his love wane after a few days?

Will this demented group get some girl into Raghav's life? What were their plans? Who would help me out of this situation?

CHAPTER 6

I collected a lot of e-documents, routines and algorithms from the dead or destroyed droid's electronic chips. Though practically every algorithm writer writes his own code, and there are a lot of similarities between codes written by two persons to perform a task, there are minor 'quirks' or signatures. Every software programmer has an ego and keeps some signature in the code.

A person may use a certain documentation technique, or he may organize routines in a certain manner. When you have organizations, then you have routines stored in common libraries. Programmers would get the routines from these company libraries and use again and again. And in addition, people store their names or initials in some places when they make a modification or when a change is done. Well, to cut the chase short, there are ways to know some details of the programmer or organization, from the codes.

The problem with droids is that, so prolific is the piracy that the codes become public in a few day's time. Entire libraries of software could become public and be available in a matter of seconds. The possibility that most of the code was pirated, and we were left with a wrong trace or we were chasing the wrong set of people or organization was huge.

So why did I collect this data? The technology used was very new. Since the droid was not pirated yet, there had to be routines that were written specifically for this droid, and I hoped to find some signature here. It was a shot in the dark.

Suvi was tired of being in the room. I had told her to walk out or see some sights, but she did not want to go anywhere by herself. So I decided that we would go for a walk. The codes could wait. A walk in Central park would be refreshing. But she wanted to know the details, and I told her whatever I could. The mood turned somber as I gave some details. We hugged each other and just lay for some time. Then I again suggested we go for a walk. She agreed

The atmosphere was too somber for any lovemaking.

We walked to Central Park. The small park in the centre of town is a solace for young lovers. Since its very early days, girls and boys used to meet here, away from the eyes of the khap panchayats that used to rule outer Delhi. These Khap Panchayats had ordered many lynching's of lovers, who belonged to different communities and stuff like that. Though the khap panchayats are no longer there, this place has retained its romantic flavor.

We sat in a corner and watched some birds on trees. Suvi wanted to go to Palika Bazaar. I was surprised considering that we still had unopened packages of undergarments and fun stuff from last evening's shopping. However, I obliged her.

We walked into Palika bazaar.

One thing about Palika bazaar is that it is difficult to locate the same shop that you visited last evening. It is what is called 'bhool bhulaiya' in Hindi or a 'maze' where you could get lost. We could not locate the shop from last evening and had to wander a bit, trying to locate it. Meanwhile, Suvi had seen a couple of retro salvar kameez with a different pattern than last evening, and we haggled and shopped.

"This way we will have to get another bag. We are buying so many things here." Suvi has a nice way of asking me to get a bag.

We walked a bit more and found our shop. The shopkeeper beamed a big smile.

"Welcome sir and madam."

He ushered us in. This time more confident than last visit, showing us more bedroom-wear. Suvi walked around and soon the shopkeeper got a couple of latex dresses and masks. I got that Suvi had fancied the same and hence the reason we were here. And this was the same retinal algorithm at work.

A seedy looking character entered the shop.

"Satsriakal bhai." he greeted the shop keeper.

Sat Sri Akal is the standard salutation of the Sikh community.

The shopkeeper acknowledged.

"You will not believe what I have with me today."

"What could it be?"

"It is the latest software from SN Droids."

"What will I do with it? I can sell droids here, but what will I do with the software?"

"You can upgrade any SN droid with this software. And the droid will perform new routines."

"Don't waste my time."

"Just try it once. It has some mind-blowing routines."

I was intrigued. I knew that routine upgrades were possible for droids. But I did not know that a grey market for the same existed.

"How much?" I asked.

The shopkeeper looked at me and then at the seedy sales guy.

Suvi asked "Why do you want it? We do not have any droids."

"For the case." I told her.

The shopkeeper named the price. I was sure that he had added his margin, whatever that was. Still well within my affordable limit.

I went to the hotel room and checked the software. It had a lot of routines. Each routine started with a copyright statement.

"This software is the property of SN corporation. No part of it may be reproduced without the written consent of SN corporation.

RGV."

I did a search by pressing Ctrl and F and typed in RGV. RGV appeared in many places in the software. The revision histories were marked as 'rgv' in small letters and main routines in Caps.

On a random thought, I opened one of the files from the Bhudevi droid and searched RGV

I found many instances.

I felt excited. Was RGV the maker of our robot's routines? Could SN be the enterprise behind all this?

It could be a coincidence.

I called Sachchit and informed him of the development.

"RGV is Ravi G Vibi. He is my equivalent in SN corporation. Vibi is very intelligent but also very straightforward. I have met him on a couple of occasions."

"Could SN be behind this?"

"SN is one of the top five corporate's in this world. It is a market leader in making sex droids. It has the resources to make this droid. We can talk with Raghav and approach their corporate to find out if they have made it for someone."

Nadir looked at Wish.

"So now they have the scent of SN organization."

"Yes."

"I think we have done our bit."

"Yes. The world will be a better place without such super powers."

"What of Raghav? Can he find a place in the council?"

"He seems to be strong, conscientious and compassionate. But does he have the will to put everything else behind for the betterment of the world? Will he be able to play the politics for keeping the world safe from within?"

"Only time can tell."

CHAPTER 7

Though people would like to think of complex plots and twists and turns in committing a crime. Sometimes, it is the simplest that create history. The abduction and what was to be done was scripted according to a simple plot. A plot that had been written by one of the best scriptwriters.

Show the intensity of DM's love, show Raghav as someone fickle and one who would soon lose interest in Bhudevi. They hoped that Bhudevi would fall apart due to this. It was only a matter of time.

And as in every plot, there are subplots. SharpNails had other secret plans. She wanted to utilize this period of Bhudevi's captivity to record Raghav and Bhudevi's sexual details. Their responses, how they behaved and so on.

Bhudevi lost track of time. She must have slept for ten or twelve hours. She was famished. Did she sleep through a meal?

As per the plot, the next phase of the plot started. The TV would play when Bhudevi was awake. Bhudevi watched a video where DM clothed a Bhudevi droid. She saw the minute attention that DM paid while dressing the droid. It gave her goose pimples, just watching the video. She and Raghav loved each other and did some things for each other. But this was too much and that too with a droid!

She saw videos of DM in deep despair and depressed when she had refused his overtures.

Then she saw videos of how he accepted the droids from SN corporation, and slowly he had returned to his normal life.

She understood that DM loved her, but it scared her too.

Finally, she could no longer take the videos. A partition opened, and a droid brought her breakfast. She ate, and that felt better. She had taken some training on how to behave in the event she was kidnapped, especially as Raghav was becoming rich and important. However, she had never imagined that it would happen in real life.

She walked out into the garden. The sky was artificial, and the plants and trees were genetically modified and grown in this artificial atmosphere. The dome had many layers of a polymer with some gas in between them. By changing the electrical supply, the gas could change colours and shapes and create a kaleidoscopic sky. It was a marvel to watch. She was lost in watching the changing sky. She, in fact, lost sense of her present predicaments.

"Do you like it?"

DM's voice brought her to reality.

"Look DM sir," she could not forget her respect for this man. "I understand that you love me. But this is not right. You have no right to do this." She had known this man in the past and felt comfortable talking with him. Whatever be the misunderstanding, this could be cleared very fast. DM was quite a reasonable man and a very important person in society. He could not do anything wrong.

"Bhudevi, you cannot possibly fathom my love for you. See all this and much more can be yours. You need not be living that paltry life. You can be a superstar. Nobody understands this business like us. Why do you deny yourself all this?"

"DM! Don't think for one moment that Raghav could not give me this. He offered to open his own studios and make movies exclusively for me. However, I want to prove my skill without being in a protected umbrella."

DM was infuriated by her mentioning Raghav. Why did she have to bring him into this conversation?

"How childish of you my dear! Be with us and you will realize your true potential."

"Be a caged bird in your golden prison? Ha Ha. Whoever gave you the idea that I would be happy here, must be out of their mind.

I would be happier in a small home with no career than in a place like this. Raghav is what I need. More than any success in career."

DM could not bear the mention of Raghav any longer and walked away. She got a glimpse of the east side. It looked like some more rooms on one side and there was a faint smell of a sea breeze.

'The best thing to do under this circumstance is to pray', She thought, and she started chanting the Ram Raksha Stotra. It gave her strength. She was reminded of the travails of Sita when Ravana had imprisoned Sita. She prayed and also said some lines from the Hanuman Chalisa prayer.

Food arrived. The droids used a door that was at the side of the room, and she could see more rooms and a galley. She ate her food and decided to rest. Save her energy and plan her escape. After a small rest, she would jog in the garden.

Her sleep was interrupted by Raghav's voice. The video was showing Raghav playfully talking with a young girl. She saw the girl touching Raghav.

She felt infuriated.

How could he?

Here I am, thwarting all advances from a person who genuinely loves me, but Raghav is flirting with this girl. Suddenly, a small movement of Raghav's hand caught her attention.

Was it like a robot? She tried to stare and see if this was a droid. She could not be sure. Her feelings of jealousy were clouding her senses.

She could not bear to watch.

But she wanted to be sure that this was not some trick. She realized that there were tears in her eyes, and that was causing some difficulty in seeing the video. She wiped these tears away.

Was all this programmed?

Was it something that DM had done?

She could not be sure. However, the person in the video did look like Raghav and not a droid.

She decided to do her walking and some stretch exercises. She had to maintain her figure and her sanity. Physical exercise helped her regain her composure. She needed to watch these videos with a balanced head. Else her mind would play games with her.

DM entered the garden.

So they were watching her, she summarized.

"Bhudevi, sorry to have hurt you, but I have been following Raghav for a long time. He is not what he seems to be. This was not the only girl whom he has flirted with. There are many. I do not want to disturb your emotions by showing you everything."

Bhudevi decided to play along.

"DM I was most disturbed by those videos. How come he never talked about this girl flirting with him? I must certainly ask him."

"He has been lying to you all this time. He has denied you, my true love. If you ask him, he will but deny. Have you asked yourself, why is this girl flirting with him? Is it because of a previous relationship? Ask yourself difficult questions to realize the truth.

It is easy to find no fault with the people you love. And very difficult to doubt them. However, unless you seek the truth, you can never be sure that the happiness you have is true. You must open your eyes!"

"I see your point. Then I must catch him myself to know that he has betrayed my trust."

"How naive of you! He is most clandestine about his affairs. Only the best detectives in the world could access this video."

"DM, you will understand that you have compromised your own situation by bringing me here.

If I tell Raghav about me discovering his affairs, them he will ridicule me. He will ask me

Where did you see it? At DM's place. When did you see it? When DM held me in captivity.

Do you see my dilemma? I cannot accost him with this evidence.

You must release me. I will accost him with this evidence, and then we shall see." Dangling a bit of hope at the end of her sentence.

"Bhudevi, you do not have to accost him. This was just to show you the truth. He has no rights over you. You have no binding. You are not married to him and do not need a divorce. Just be mine."

"But DM, I have a binding with him. I must clear my conscience that I have acted properly. I must give him a chance to explain. You see DM; you do not understand. This is not a logical or legal or business matter. It is emotional. I Must clear things with Raghav. Just let me go for a few days and let me sort matters with him."

"So you are not ready to believe me."

"I must give Raghav a chance to clear himself."

"No you need not."

"But I must!"

"No. And that is final." DM was not used to people questioning his authority. Bhudevi started crying.

"Bhudeviji It is not my intention to hurt you or make you cry. But for us to live happily ever after."

"That will never happen." Somewhere something in her snapped and she gave vent to her feelings.

"You still do not believe me."

"I know Raghav. He will never betray me. All these videos have been cooked by you."

"Very well! Have it your way. You have time till my birthday to make up your mind and be mine happily. Else irrespective of your state of mind, I will make you mine. For your own good!

Sometimes people are their own enemies and have to be rescued from themselves."

This continued for a few days. Then her Raghav droid was brought in. She felt that this Raghav droid was her companion droid that she had brought with her. She conversed with the droid. She asked questions that she wanted answers to. She hoped that some circuit in the droid could convey some of these messages to Raghav. SN was watching her every move. It was her suggestion that the droid be introduced into her life.

At night, she saw the Raghav droid make sexual advances towards her. She was aroused.

In SharpNails control room, Sharpnail could sense the rise in Bhudevi's body temperature. She started the scanner and soon a set of sensors were capturing Bhudevi's breathing pattern and her temperature profile. Generally, when she had cooperative celebrities, the ones who had signed up for making their droids, she had special probes and tools inserted, and then she had a special dildo that would be inserted, and the sex would start, and she would capture the celebrity's signature. But here she had no such facilities.

Within seconds, Bhudevi regained her sense of where she was and soon got up from bed. She and Raghav rarely used the droids for such purposes. There had been an occasional session, when they were away from each other for weeks. However, Raghav and she had a pact that there had to be the other person at the other end. Else it would be breaking their moral code.

SharpNails saw Bhudevi get up. That dud! Why don't you just enjoy this and let me get your sex signature?

At least, she had a better knowledge of Bhudevi's responses. She needed more information from Raghav, and then she could do a classical 'man in the middle' kind of cyber attack and get all required information. The only way would be to seek such responses from Raghav's Bhudevi droid at the other end. So she programmed the Bhudevi droid in Tholus to start making more sexual demands. Raghav did not realize that it was not Bhudevi, and she got some of his signatures and programmed the same into the Raghav droid.

This complex cyclical process of capturing Raghav's responses through the Bhudevi droid and passing it to Bhudevi and capturing her responses and passing to the Bhudevi droid in Tholus was slow. The progress being made with Bhudevi was slower. Bhudevi started responding positively at times. She allowed the Raghav droid to do things beneath the bedsheets! How naïve! However, Bhudevi did not go all the way.

SN was going crazy with the slow progress.

Go Girl! Go ahead and give me your signature! Why the f*#k isn't DM just going and banging this girl and letting me get the signatures! What was so special about her?! What is special about any woman, including me?

My droids have the best organs in the world. So many advancements, that even god did not make into women. Billions are hooked to sex with my droids. They have stopped doing it to any woman. Why risk disease and do so many things while a better experience awaits them with their sex droid. Droids that never lose their shape and never smell bad. The auto flush sequence that I have loaded into every droid cleans their organs to surgical precision. In fact, the process and organs are UFDA certified. The thousand tongues technology inside the female droid organs creates such a sensation, that men cannot withstand it even for a few minutes! Who but I could imagine this 'combination' sex.

I am not god but what god has created, I have perfected!

CHAPTER 8

For an ordinary person, it would have been very difficult to contact Vibi. However, Sachchit was no ordinary person. Sachchit was the originator, the pioneer of the Droid business.

He showed his college project of making a companion droid to Raghav, and that is how it all started.

Raghav had seen the pain caused to his mother when his father had expired. This personal tragedy made him see the advantage of having companion droids. Sachchit still remembered those initial days: These droids needed a lot of personal information and had to be personally sold. So they, Sachchit and Raghav, worked out an elaborate scheme.

Their sales and marketing team generally located couples who were married or had committed long-term relationships. They would then explain their concept.

The general presentation guideline was given as part of their sales training to the salespersons.

You are here today, living happily and comfortably. Confident that the other person is available in your life. He or she is there to listen to you, to talk with you. We all know that our time in this universe is limited. At some point of time, you will be faced with the option of living alone.

What happens then?

You have taken life insurance and ensured wealth to the other

But is wealth everything?

That is where Ayudham program comes in. Ayudham or tool in Tamil is what we provide you.

Once you have enrolled in this program, we will make one droid of each of you. We provide basic information about you to the corresponding droid. We have a three-day session in Ayudh labs where you will be asked to perform certain tasks and speak some things. Your mannerisms, speech, tone and habits will be programmed to the droids.

Then the droids would be provided to you. With each passing day, the droid keeps learning about you and at any point when the other person is not there you can use the droid as your companion. That is you do not have to wait for a long time, but you can start right away.

Now what other things are our droids capable of? They are security trained. You need not worry about your security. They remind you of doors that need locking, closing your lockers at home and the key is stored in a compartment that is sealed during a security threat.

Our droids can also act as a music station and have a 3d holographic projector. With enrolment to this program, you will have access to our library of more than 30000 movies at any point of time.

The droids come equipped with knowledge from our online encyclopedia, which is now acknowledged to be the biggest in the world.'

Started small and they led the Droid industry for quite some time.

Sachchit and Vibi had met on many occasions in different seminars on droids, and both appreciated each other's knowledge and skills on droids. They were both avant-garde programmers and could envision the next generation of droids. Naturally, there was also a kind of secret race between them.

While Raghav's organization and hence Sachchit focused on companion droids, Vibi's organization focused on the sex side. However, each advancement in one kind of droid, made the other think of the next improvement. There was a lot of respect for the other's skills.

Sachchit called Vibi's direct number.

"Hi. Sachchit. Been a long time."

"Hi Vibi. Yes. After the Tholus seminar, we have not met since then."

"Yes. So how come?"

"Vibi, I needed your help."

"Sure Sachchit." Vibi was suddenly warm. Sachchit asking his help was something that he could be proud of and tell others.

"Vibi, we are dealing with a Bhudevi Droid. It is very-very advanced. It has .1 X .1 cell size. Would you have any idea about it?"

"Hi Sachchit, I do not know what you are talking about." Vibi lied. How had Sachchit come to know about this droid? How did he get hold of it?

"Vibi. The software has your signature all over it."

"Sachchit, it is possible that some pirate has copied my routines. I cannot say until I look over this thing. Can you send it to my labs?" Vibi was guarded.

I felt that this cat and mouse talk had gone too far. Time for someone to talk straight and get some answers.

"Vibi," I interrupted, "I am Anjani, and I work for Sugriv. We are a small outfit. I am here because Bhudevi has been kidnapped and has been replaced by this self-destructing droid. We know for sure that it has all the markings of SN droids. The software has your signatures.

We could have gone to the galactic police, because we believe that this goes beyond this planet. However, we are sure that you can throw some light on who ordered this droid and for whom. This will save us a lot of trouble and gain us time.

Bhudevi could be in great danger. Her life hangs on the speed with which you answer our questions. I am sorry to have interrupted your conversation with Sachchit."

"See Vibi, we need your help in this matter." Sachchit interrupted.

Raghav started in a chocked voice "Vibi, I do not want you to compromise any secret of your organization. Neither am I interested in any of your software routines nor secrets." The software and the droid were really advancements that needed to be guarded by SN. These routines and developments would take billions in R&D expenses and save billions to a competing organization.

"I just want Bhudevi back." Raghav's voice cracked, and he started sobbing like a child.

People moved, brought him water to drink immediately.

Vibi's mind was confused. He had his loyalty to his organization, and he was faced with a moral dilemma on the other hand. He felt that his skills had been exploited for wrong purposes by his organization. He was the second in command to SN. Though he would always remain the technical head of the organization, SN was the business head. He was very happy with this arrangement. He had always been proud of the fact that he was trusted enough to know that DM had had a crush on Bhudevi, and he was entrusted of making Bhudevi droids. The budgets for making these were never limited. It helped him improve the quality of droids for the general populace.

"Sachchit, I am bound by my company's secrecy rules. You know all this." Vibi said.

I felt that was the first acknowledgement that they had indeed made the Bhudevi droid. What a breakthrough in this case!

"I understand this Vibi." Sachchit answered. "Believe me, if the kidnapping had not happened, I would have only felt that someone was making the best of droids, much better than we are making and appreciated the work. Even now technically, I believe that this is the best droid, I have seen till date, and we are ages behind this droid. But this kidnapping has forced us to ask."

I thought Vibi needed some moral assurance. He would break. "Vibi, do you want to be assisting some kidnapper? Maybe even a murderer!"

"No, certainly not."

"Vibi, we only need to know who has ordered it and for whom. Your name would never appear anywhere." Raghav chipped in. "Once Bhudevi is located and rescued. I will be indebted to you. After looking at this droid, I am certain that we have a long way to go in the sex droid business. We will probably exit that business, and that would make you the champion in that field. Your organization would be indebted to you."

"I'm not sure of that. When they know that I am the one who has informed, then I am finished."

"Why do you say that? I have met SN and am sure that she will understand why I had to ask you and why you had to reply."

"That's because SN ordered it and for DM."

We were all stunned by this revelation. Everything fell in place. Definitely, Kumb was involved in the making of the movie. Perhaps Meghnath too was involved. And SharpNails must have made the Droid, and DM must have ordered the switch. I did not want to put this into such words. I mean like we were talking about the 'Who's who' in today's Galaxy. DM, SN, Kumb and Meghnath featured among the top fifty richest persons in the world.

"Thanks Vibi. We will discuss with DM and enquire about Bhudevi. We will not name you, but will only seek her return."

"I think there could be some reprisal against me."

"The moment you are questioned or feel that your situation would be compromised, just take the nearest route to any of my offices, and you will be taken care of. However, I do not think such a situation will arise."

Raghav spoke out. "Due to the gravity of the situation, I have to talk with DM."

Raghav had one of DM's cards. Ones that CEO's give to CEO's. DM called the number and reached DM's secretary.

"Good Morning. This is DM's office. How may I help you today?"

"Good Morning. This is Raghav. I need to talk with DM."

"I'm sorry sir. He is out of office. I will send him a message."

"It is very urgent. Can you tell me where I can reach him?"

"OK. I will check his 'out of office' message." There was a pause as they heard some music. "Sir, it says that he is in an SN Droid conference and is not to be disturbed. However, I will send him a message."

"OK." Raghav started thinking about alternative routes of action.

"Let me go to SN corporation headquarters. I will accost them and seek out Bhudevi's address." I offered.

"SN corporation headquarters is in one of the islands in the Indian ocean. It is an approximately 30 square kilometer in size. They have their research laboratories and some of the smaller-scale production facilities there.

Two adjacent islands with some 100 sq kilometer areas house their factories serving earth.

Their Mega facilities are in Mars. These facilities serve the entire galaxy other than earth.

The enterprise here is known as SN Droid earth corporation limited. And the one in Mars is known as SN Droid Galaxy corporation.

The laws for galaxy and earth in some matters of the droids are different." Sachchit offered.

"Raghavji, just give me one of your jet packs and let me make a quick visit." I urged. "There is no time to waste." Raghav had a set of jet packs. These packs were still in the ultra-rich domain. Many governments in earth were afraid that these could not be handed over to the general populace. Some countries completely banned jet packs and their use. However, India was one of the few that allowed the Jet packs by special approval of the government. So the top few and the ultra rich in India had jet packs. There were a lot of red tape on the usage of jet packs. The source and destination had to be registered, a flight path approved, and you could then use the same. It took a few hours to get that done.

"OK. I'll call my flight station to keep things ready for you."

Suvi was not happy that I was going alone on this assignment. I was not happy that I was going alone. My entire plan to use this week to start my backlog on the variable ramp and practice my "Hammer the G spot" technique had not materialized. In fact, I was without Suvi most of the time. I told the details in brief.

"Will Raghav accept Bhudevi after she returns?" Her question astounded me.

"You are watching too many soap serials on TV." I quipped. "Of course he will. He is absolutely desolate without Bhudevi."

"Don't blame the soap serials. They show the truth about human relationships. I have seen in many serials that men have difficulty to accept a woman after she has an affair with someone else or some such episodes."

It is absolute stupidity to stand between a woman and her favorite TV soap serials. I hugged Suvi and assured her. "I have seen Raghav and seen how desperate he is to have Bhudevi back. So do not worry."

"Take care. You do not know these super rich. They will forget you once you are out of their sight."

"I will take care of myself. And I will take extra precautions, not because I am on an assignment for Raghav, but because, I am on assignment here and then to Bhimtal for your sake . . ." I tried to add some cheer.

She blushed. I felt she was ready . . . I was ready too. I thought that I could waste a couple of hours being with and within Suvi. After all in such a situation, even god may not know, what god has planned for me.

CHAPTER 9

The Jet pack station was ready by the time I reached there. The Jet pack was almost an aircraft in itself. I was not exposed to the climate like in the ancient comic books. It had many parts; the actual nuclear fuel propelled drive, the helmet and body armor that was in two parts. One for the lower body and one for the upper. There was a limited motion that was possible. The source and destination were programmed. I was also explained the manual mode of piloting.

The brief on the operation of the jet pack took almost 45 minutes. It was almost evening. That had been a somewhat long session with Suvi.

After the flight technical team had finished the final checks, they gave their 'OK' to the flight. The flight was auto programmed to go to SN corporation island. The jet was programmed to avoid most of the inhabited places. I flew over various offshore rigs that served as homes now. After a few hours of the same sea, sea, ships, ships, rig homes, I came to more open sea. I must have dozed off. I woke up and looked, luckily the autopilot thing kept me straight-on course. After some time, I could see some of the islands that SN corporation owned. Some of the islands were fabled to have been made with golden roads, and I could see some that looked almost golden from a distance. I was tempted to have a look at them. Maybe on my way back.

I docked into their flight room. My Jet pack was stored in a locker made for the same. I was handed a token. A nice young nubile looking woman arrived. She looked at me with an invitingly. The waiting room was big and had couches.

"Anything I can do for Anjani san.:"

"I am here for an urgent meeting with Madam SharpNails or Mr. DM."

"Mr. DM is out in another place. He will be flying later to come here to meet you. You must wait here. I take good care of you. Make you relax before the meeting."

"I'm 'OK' thank you."

"I make you more 'OK'."

I did not want to be more 'OK'. "Thank you. But I think I will sleep." She giggled. Soon, there were two more girls. They brought my change of clothes. I started to take the clothes.

"No Anjani san, you must let us serve you." The girls were already giggling. I was undressed by the girls. As they unbuttoned my shirt, their fingers sliding, touching my chest, nipples, tummy, ever so lightly. Creating ripples of sensation. I did not want to let them touch my pants. This was too much to bear. I moved backwards and fell on a couch. The girls started giggling and laughing.

"No. Enough." I mustered some morality and said. My voice sounding hoarse.

"Why so afraid, Anjani San? Suvi never find out. This is only company . . . offer relaxation."

"It is a moral question. You may not understand."

The girls were already seated. They were touching my pants, pleading looks.

"Let us do our duty, Anjani San." One of them pleaded.

"Our boss be very angry, we not serve you good. Anjani san. Please be cooperate." Their fingers ever so subtly touching my crotch. My pants were on fire. Expertly, they removed my pants. I was already pinned down by Miss Japan. I got my 'best experience' blow job.

"Oh Anjani san, why so soon?" The two girls now giggling. The heat was so high, my forehead sweating. I was breathless.

"You no give us much time. You must give us too much time."

"Enough. I said enough." I cried out hoarsely.

"You say enough, but your man say, 'More. More.'" Now all of them giggling.

One of the girls pressed a button, and one of the couches moved away revealing a Jacuzzi bath tub. The water was hot and inviting. The girls asked me to move into the bath tub. The water pressure relaxing my muscles. The few hours long journey on the Jet pack had created some tiredness. The girls gave an ever so light massage. I was lost in a series of 'waves of pleasure'. I was so tired that I could literally not get up from the

Jacuzzi. The girls helped me up and put me on the bed. I must have dozed quite heavily.

When I woke up, it was morning. The girls came in, and I had another bath in the Jacuzzi. Luckily, this time they did not do things that would make me question my morality. Breakfast was served.

"Mr. DM and Miss SharpNails, now ready to receive you."

"Thank you." Finally, I was going to accost them.

I was walked into a room that was almost like a small theater. There were several droid models in the room. DM and SharpNails were impeccably dressed.

"Ah! Hello Mr. Anjani. I have heard a lot about you." SN giggled.

"I hope your evening was comfortable." DM chipped in.

"Yes. Thank you for your hospitality."

"You re welcome. When I came to know that you are going to visit us, I left my other activities as soon as I could and rushed in here." DM said. So businesslike and professional. I knew I had to be tough. Somehow all this sweetness had to melt away, and we had to be at each other's throats. That's how you deal with ruffians. These people were ruffians of a different type. You have to take away their mask and let them come down on you screaming and shouting.

"Let's cut the crap." I started in a brazen way. "We know that you have Bhudevi in your custody somewhere. You have kidnapped her. We want her returned." I wanted to surprise them.

DM laughed out loudly. SN joined in.

"Anjani, had you not come from Raghav's enterprise, we would have thrown you out for making this accusation. We have done nothing like that. We do not know where Bhudevi is, and we certainly do not intend to get accused like this."

"DM, you cannot hide like a rat. You have done something that you cannot be proud of. We have your Bhudevi droid, made by SN enterprises. We have your plot unearthed."

"Then why is it that you have come here to accuse me of all this? Why have you not approached the police? Certainly, you know where she is or have some complaint from her."

"I have documented evidence that it was you who ordered the Droid be made, and that it be replaced for the real Bhudevi. This is abduction of the worst kind that you have done. You are so afraid of Raghav, and his strength that you have chosen to behave like a rat."

DM was not used to be talked to like this. SN also was jolted by this brazen attack by Anjani. They had been surrounded for ages by people who idolized them. SN did not want matters to get out of hands.

"I know that you have been informed so by Vibi. We immediately removed him from our organization." They had spent the last evening, where they had personally gone and Vibi was accosted by DM, DM holding Vibi's collar back as he was unceremoniously taken to the security gates. Vibi's career was finished. He had no right to reveal the company's secrets.

"You may think that you are very smart. However, you do not know the strength and vision that Raghav has. He will have the last laugh. You have made grave errors, the consequences of which you may not fathom now. All is not lost. Return Bhudevi with all respect and we will not seek revenge."

"Revenge. What do you think you guys are? Do you even know where Bhudevi is? You guys are just shouting into the wind. So what are you going to say? That you have some damaged droid. That the droid was made in SN. So what! The world knows that SN corporation makes the best droids. It could be a business competition matter. The press in the world will see it that way. And what else will you say?

That Bhudevi was abducted?

By whom?

By Me?

Who will believe you?

What is there to say that Bhudevi has not left of her own accord? Can you see the scandal that it will brew? Bhudevi fights with Raghav and leaves him and lives with DM.

I could have a Bhudevi droid appear anywhere and declare that she has abandoned Raghav. Nobody will believe you guys.

You have nothing!

You have lost Bhudevi and know that there is nothing that you can do about it.

You can go and tell your boss, that Bhudevi is no longer his. If he desires, I will send the best Bhudevi droid for him to enjoy. However, the real Bhudevi will be mine."

From DM's perspective, I was puny non-entity. He had agreed to his guilt, but I had no ways of proving it in a court of law.

"What you have done DM, is cross the boundaries that you should not have caused. Be warned that you will suffer due to this."

"Suffer! You do not know what suffering is. I will teach you guys the lesson of your lifetime. You saw my hospitality yesterday. You could have had a longer stay here and enjoyed my hospitality and experienced women and luxuries beyond your imagination. You had to be polite and respectful. That's all."

"Polite! Towards you! Your wealth has gone to your head. You do not respect humanity anymore. You have crossed the boundary that humans have seldom done in their history on this planet. You are bringing untold suffering to yourself. You still have time to come out of your grandiose vision about yourself and accept your mistake and seek Raghav's pardon. Return Bhudevi and repent!" I was taken aback by the strength in my own voice. However, somewhere in his arrogance, DM had forgotten that I was also a respected member of my community. I may not be a king and as rich as DM, but I had my own life and pleasures. And he had done something that all men fear and despise. Steal their spouse!

"You arrogant bastard!" DM's language slipped. I was sure that this is where I wanted him to be. This is where he would make the mistakes, that would ultimately lead us to victory. What mistakes? I was not sure what they would be.

"I will have you imprisoned in this island. Teach you how to behave." DM pressed a button. Three ruffians came in. I was prepared for a fight. One of them fired a stun gun from a distance, and I was tazed with a high-voltage pulse. I was soon handcuffed.

"Keep him in the barracks with the general populace for two days and then let him go." DM ordered.

The three guards took me to a 'open air' ground surrounded by walls. The area was lightly guarded by security guards. On one side were some rooms. Maybe people relaxed there. People were playing football, volleyball and some games. It was a small 'open' prison in that island.

I wondered, if they were allowed to have a prison in their islands. The people who were looking at me, started walking around me. My handcuffs were released, and I was free to walk. I looked and found a few friendly faces. I smiled, and they smiled back.

"Hi." One of them said. His name was Greg. He looked European.

"Hi." We introduced ourselves.

"So how come?" He enquired why I was here.

"DM has imprisoned someone. I came to request DM to release. We got into a heated argument. And so I am here." I summarized the reason."

"You argued with DM!" There was a look of incredulity on his face.

"So what? To me, he is nothing but a rich criminal. Not like my boss Raghav." I retorted.

"You work for Raghav?"

"Yes. Actually, I work for Sugriv and am on loan to help Raghav find this missing person. Who are you and how come you are here?" Some of the people had overheard that I had had an argument with DM and had collected around us.

"I am one of the stem cell experts whom they hired from Europe. I was doing a lot of research for DM and SN from Europe, and they wanted me to move to the core of their enterprise.

I was very eager to move in here. But once I reached here, I found out the way they were getting their stem cells.

They hire a lot of young women from around the world. The women get impregnated with the best of semen from the world. Then in two or three months time, the umbilical cord is already having the stem cells that they require. The woman is aborted, and the cycle continues. The stem cells generate a lot of wealth for SN.

The women are paid well. However, they go through 3-4 abortions in a year. They are fed special steroids to quicken the process. There has been no study on the effects of the usage of these steroids.

There are some women, who do not want to get aborted. The abortion was, is and will be a huge challenge to women. However, SN has no option but go this way until they find a way to create artificial wombs that can hold children in them. That is a long way away.

I objected to this way of obtaining stem cells. The whole world believes that SN makes their stem cells. However, this is the gory truth. They do make a lot of things once the stem cells are available. Most of the research is a collaboration of SN's global teams. I do not want to demean or put down some of SN's achievements. However, this method seems unethical to me."

"Don't the women object?" I asked.

"No. Most of these women are looking for an easy way to make a living. Many have left children behind, in their home towns, who need to be looked after. Money has to be sent home. You will be surprised on how a community of people start accepting this way of living as a norm.

There will be women, who counsel and tell the others that this is what they have to do to make a living. Women counsel, who will guide them to be more productive to make more money, and the cycle continues. Most of the women will find that once they start earning more, their families needs in the other world increases. They end up in a cycle of endless demands from their families. Slowly, they end up signing larger contracts and taking part in other enterprises, that they would not otherwise have worked in." He insinuated the adult movie enterprise.

"It's nauseating."

"The men and women who oppose these methods are made to be in the prison. Where we do nothing but play volleyball and football and chess and what not. After a few days, most people realize that they are wasting their days away, earning the minimum basic pay and spending on food and other essentials, while their families need the weekly and monthly bonuses and make a compromise. You see, we earn the minimum of basic salary and other facilities. Barely enough to make us meet our daily needs. Everything is performance bonuses.

And believe me that these bonuses are very big. I objected and was brought here. Believe me, there are people who are at the other end earning their bonuses and think that I am their enemy.

But I think that this abortion business is wrong."

"So why do you not complain?"

"To whom? These groups of islands are a public enterprise governed by the World private nations act. This is not part of a democratic country, but a private country owned by DM and his gang. If I raise a voice, there will be a hundred who will shout against me. And what DM or SN is doing, is not illegal. Even in other parts of the world. Today mothers have a right to choose to abort. That is recognized by 100% of the countries of the world.

The world has not seen the industrialization of abortions for the stem cell and droid industry.

Raghav's droids are more expensive and more ethical. I realize that now. Initially, I used to wonder, why this corporate had such a skewed cost structure. Now I know the truth. Raghav gets his stem cells from the discarded umbilical waste. He is not manufacturing them as it is done here. His droid business is also more focused on companionship. More like a once a lifetime Droid."

"So what do we do now." I thought that there are many injustices in the world. This was one more to that list. However, I had other things on top of my mind.

"When I go out, I will file a petition seeking the abolition of the industrialized abortion. However, I know that I have signed a contract that would violate secrecy agreements with SN corporation. They could have me imprisoned. I will move from one prison to another." Ha Ha. He laughed a hollow laugh.

I saw that he was an idealist. The world needs people like these. People who think differently and may bring the world to see some of its mistakes.

"Contact me when you are out. I will put in a word with Raghav."

"Yes. That is still a year away."

"Not if we can escape this prison."

"Escape where? Swim a thousand miles to the nearest country. And most Asian countries will not readily make enemies with SN. SN sources their women from many Asian, Arabic and African countries. They see recruitment from SN as a steady source of foreign exchange. Nobody will take you in. You will not get press coverage, and no courts will accept your appeals.

I doubt even the European and American countries would do this today. Especially with the precarious world economy position.

They are always afraid that DM may move his business to the other planets or other celestial bodies under his control. We know that there are costs involved. However, the countries will not risk that."

I looked around. We had a small group of people who were near us.

"Don't worry about this group. We are all like a family. A community that hates what's going on in this island."

"I have a jet pack in the security gate." I searched my pockets and found the token. I showed it to Greg.

"Hmmm. Well, it looks like if you reach the security, you have a chance to go away. But watch out, they could have tampered with your jet pack."

"I have to take my chances. Do you have any ideas?"

One of the women came forward. She looked a bit fat. I looked at her odd body structure.

"She is six months into pregnancy. She came here after she objected to her abortion. Well anyway, they got her abortion done. Then she met with a security guard here, and they fell in love. This is their baby." People will be people. She was trying to hide her pregnancy and hence looked so odd.

"I will ask Mohan to help us." That was the name of the security guard. "But please never tell anything about this to anyone. Mohan has a wife and two children in India. He has to send them money regularly. He cannot risk being seen involved in any of this. I have given my word to him (about keeping her baby a secret)."

"OK. Thanks. I will not speak about Mohan." I assured her.

Mohan was in the night shift. The pregnant woman talked with Mohan, and he agreed to let me escape through one of the gates in the west. This was very near the entrance Security gates. The escape would have to be planned at around 6 AM or just before that. The guards change shifts at 6:00 Am. So 5:45 onwards, there is some reporting that they have to do. Mohan would leave the gate unlocked and then move to the main security office for the handover. Due to this being an island, security guards were slack. Where would anyone escape? No one had attempted an escape before this, and they thought that no one would ever be able to do so for ever.

And this would also be the best time to get the Jet pack. Chances that the story of my arrest had not reached the first shift guards were high. So I slept lightly. I woke up at around 5:00 AM. I used the public bath and toilet available in those premises.

At 5:45 I was near the gate where Mohan was stationed. Mohan moved to the main security gate. I walked towards the gate. Soon I was outside the gate. I was immediately onto a beach. I kept as close to the walls as possible and started walking towards the main building. I had forgotten that I would be outside and had to enter the main security building. This was a flaw in our plan. I did not know how I would make it into the building. Mohan had informed that this route did not have cameras. I reached the main security building around 6:00 AM. I could see a few women swimming in the sea. They were either naked or had very minimum clothes. I hit upon an idea. I took off my clothes and hid them near the front door and went in for a swim.

After a small swim, I walked to the entrance. And stood there in my birthday suit, my clothes near the entrance door, where the guard could not see. And smiled at the Security guard. He looked at me with disdain. And opened the door. I quickly collected my clothes and walked in. He pointed me to go to the toilet and get dressed. I did that and came out.

I handed him my token.

"F*#king Tourists." He muttered as he went to get my gear. I quickly thanked him and wore my outfit and moved to the docking area. I started my Jet pack. There was a sudden jerk. I was tossed out towards the sea. There was fire coming out of one of the engines.

My god, someone had tried to tamper with the jet pack. But had done a piss-poor job of doing that. The ride was unpredictable and bumpy. I was getting tossed around the island, instead of the program taking me back to Raghav's place.

I tried to take the controls to manual. It came to manual and I tried to control and got tossed to a part that looked like two giant generator sets. I tried some maneuvers, but looked like some of the controls had got badly damaged. I was suddenly tossed to a Diesel tank. The impact caused some of the diesel fumes to come out, and I thought I was going to get blown away with the tank. However, the engine started at the last fraction of the second, and I was literally thrown out to the sky by the explosion that followed. The explosion threw me at a very high height. I tried to look down and saw a huge fire. I prayed that the Jet pack should not fail again and drop me into the fire.

The controls were behaving very bad. The fire coming out of the engine was causing the bottom part of the body suit to get over heated. And some coolant was discharged by the body suit, that caused some chill. Sometimes, it would become very hot and sometimes very cold.

I was literally moving in a zig zag manner. I tried some of the controls in my hand. The ride was very bumpy. In seconds, I would be almost at sea level and in seconds, I would be very high up in the sky. I had no means of knowing where I was. The speed would become supersonic and then drop down to very low. My brain was telling me to abandon this jerky ride and start swimming. My body was aching all over. I had to tell my mind to keep going for a few more minutes. I had to reach some shore. I was not sure, of how my body would react once I reached the shores. Could I swim or not? I did not know. My body was hurting all over.

I saw a few rigs. OK, so I was reaching the shores of India soon. I did not know which town or city I would hit. I had lost total sense of where I was going. I could see the shoreline now. It looked like a small beach with a few houses. This was certainly not the city that I had left.

Suddenly, the engine conked off. I was rapidly losing height. I pressed, emergency eject button. The Jet pack disintegrated and I slowly landed in the sea with a small parachute that was part of the top body armor. The body suit had some floatation device built into it, which got filled with air. I landed on water, and the parachute was cut off. I thought, I had an arduous swim ahead.

CHAPTER 10

I started swimming towards the coast. Better conserve my energy. The floatation device actually slowed me down. I was gladly surprised to see a chopper approaching.

I tried to signal with my arms. A ladder dropped from the chopper. It was the coast guard. I was soon pulled in. I was surprised to see Raghav in the chopper. The paramedic gave me a quick check and suggested an anesthetic. I held my hand up and asked Raghav to come near.

"DM agrees that he has the person with him. But challenges us to find her." I summarized. Raghav was visibly angry.

"OK. We will talk once we are ashore."

The paramedic insisted that I needed an anesthetic and needed a CT scan and Xray. Above all, I needed rest. Raghav assured him that all this would be taken care of at Raghav's headquarters.

We reached the coast guard station and there was an ambulance waiting for us. I was quickly moved to the ambulance. It was from one of Raghav's hospitals. He owned a chain. A quick CT scan and Xray were conducted. Except some numbness in my left foot, I did not see anything abnormal. The Doctor said, "There's been some trauma. As if he has been in some extreme roller coaster. However, no damage that a night's sleep and relaxants will not set right."

That was good news. We reached Raghav's office. I was surprised when Sugriv, Vibi and Sachchit entered the room.

I quickly told Raghav and others about all that had happened. He thanked me profusely.

"Words cannot express, the gratitude that I have for your service. You have put your life into great risk, for my sake." Raghav said. I blushed. I am not very comfortable when too many compliments come my way.

However, Sugriv is Sugriv. "Let us not forget that they now know that we know. Time is moving fast against us. We have to brainstorm and find out where Bhudevi is."

"There are two places where DM has his resorts. One is here in SN islands. My first guess would have been the same. You may not be aware, but you blew up the entire power to 16 of DM's islands. He had multiple power cables going in from the main island to all these islands. Some kind of cost cutting measure. The other islands had small generators. However, they had been lying neglected for a long time.

When you blew up the Diesel tank, all the power sources were cut off. All the generators and backup were dependent on Diesel tank for their supply.

By now, all his cryo-tanks would be down. All his stem cell crops from last two years would have become unusable. There will be no more research possible for at least another six months. No more droids coming from these islands.

It is going to be a very huge financial blow to DM.

In short, Anjani, you have almost destroyed DM's financial clout." Vibi added.

"It was by accident. Their personnel had tampered with the jet Pack. Consequently, the engine emitted fire and threw me all over the island. I was lucky to escape from that diesel tank at the last moment."

"Whatever is destined to happen usually happens. You were destined to escape from that tank." Raghav added. "Luckily, no one died on the island. Sugriv, I think it is time to release some of these details of industrial-scale abortions to the press. Along with people being held in captivity."

"Good thinking Raghav." Sugriv agreed. He quickly dialed the press division and gave some details.

"Where do you think DM may have hidden Bhudevi?" Raghav asked Vibi.

"Of course DM has many locations to hide Bhudevi. However, this droid was made with a special request to keep the component's sea worthy.

In earth, DM has islands in the Indian ocean, that are now 'out of service' due to Anjani. He also has created an artificial sea in Mars. This sea was created by capturing water vapor from Titan and trapping inside a huge dome. The dome is almost hundred and sixty kilometers in length and almost same breadth. It is held up by artificially built pressure. It is wonderful technology. This main dome is surrounded by millions of domes. Each of this dome is approximately a kilometer in diameter. Each is like a home for the super rich. With droids and what not.

And DM has a huge palatial mansion there."

"Anjani, looks like your next assignment is in Mars." Sugriv added.

"Anjani has done enough. He needs some rest. We will work this out between us and lucky." Raghav added.

"I need to call Suvi and inform her that I am alright."

"Don't worry her unnecessarily. I have done that already." Sugriv informed. "She is now in Akshardham, praying for your better health. She is on a two-day package with devotees. So you have one more day to finish all this and be back with her and then continue your vacation."

Sugriv was a very tough boss to satisfy.

"I think, you Vibi, Sachchit and Sugriv need to be here and man the command center. Raghav, myself and Raghav's friend Lucky in Mars, will take care of the Mars end." I offered with as bright a smile as was possible under the circumstances.

The council met urgently within hours of the explosion in the Indian Ocean.

"So Raghav has shown some nerve!"

"DM is a smart bugger. This could already be insured or subcontracted to some of his cronies, who will become the fall person."

"The issue is, have we gone too far with DM. We need someone like DM to keep control of the underworld."

"Or we could have a new order. Some of the businesses will get erased and will remain un-explored for some time. And then someone else would arise to take care of the same."

"Or Raghav could hand over these to someone who is capable of doing things more ethically. He could bring in more accountability into the system."

"Only time can tell what happens."

"He is now tied up trying to bring back his beloved. That is a weak link. He has to get over it to make it to the council."

"Ok let us watch this as it unfolds."

"The council would end up losing a lot of money. It has invested in DM's Indian Ocean operations."

"Money, we can always make from elsewhere. Maybe we will have Raghav turn them into profitable enterprises later."

CHAPTER 11

Though there were guards and droids where Bhudevi was held, they were lax. They were super confident that she could not escape. Bhudevi, behaved quite casually, telling DM that Raghav would rescue her. Her confidence kind of relaxed DM and others.

Bhudevi could now move freely to the Pantry. She had cooked a couple of her meals there. She expressed her desire to see the sea. And DM obliged. She could walk on the beach. She could feel SN watching over her. Soon she started a jogging routine.

She saw another Bhudevi droid in the same location. It was quite by accident. She was jogging alongside the artificial beach, and SN was on the balcony watching her. When Bhudevi walked past her balcony, she chanced upon a maid bringing tea to SN. Bhudevi watched with interest as the maid was her exact replica.

SN quickly motioned the maid to go away. However, Bhudevi had seen the maid by that time. If Raghav could be fooled by a Droid, then could DM also be? She started devising escape plans. Have the droid replace her and then be in hiding. Where could she hide? She had jogged a few miles, and the beach just seemed to extend into the far beyond, with no end in sight. There was no civilization or village in sight anywhere.

Bhudevi was aware that DM's birthday was approaching. In the past, she had herself wished him and sent him presents on his birthday. That was when she was doing the movie that DM had made. Now, she did not wish to see his birthday near.

The plot that SN, Kumb, Meghnath and DM had hatched, had a profound psychological effect on Bhudevi. At times, she felt sympathetic toward DM. To be so much in love with somebody, so as to create droids of them and do the things that DM had done was touching. To say the least. At the same time, there was a desperation in him. The need to capture her and make her a captive. Sometimes her mind told her that this was also a kind of love. Why would someone want to capture and captivate someone?

However, at some point, her thoughts seemed to be a betrayal of Raghav and their love. DM and SN did not know the extent of her love for Raghav. It was her childhood and teenage love. It was not something that she could compromise on. She felt that she had betrayed Raghav by entertaining these thoughts of DM's love.

Her mind was going through all these twists and turns. At times, she felt that soon her brain would explode. And in this complex situation, she tried to keep her sanity alive and act normal. And plan an eventual getaway.

She had so far lived her life under Raghav's shade. He planned all their outings, their travels. She rarely drove and had taken for granted that Raghav would take care of that. Now even the thought of escaping was daunting. Even if she did escape, where would she go? Where was she? She had no idea. She had a terrible sense of direction and navigation.

Then two days before DM's birthday, she saw DM and SN in an agitated conversation. Their faces contorted with anger. She could hear them cursing about someone named Anjani. She knew that Anjani was a friend of Sugriv's. So Raghav was hitting back at DM. Great! She did her jog and entered her captivity room.

SN suddenly appeared there.

"Maharani!" She was obviously angry. "Your paradise days are coming to an end." Before Bhudevi could understand, two droids had appeared behind her, and she was injected with an anesthetic.

She woke up and found herself tied to a hospital bed. There were a couple of probes probing her parts and recording her internals. She was being droidized. SN was standing near the bed. She was the one who had ordered this.

Bhudevi wanted to object. "You have no right to do this."

"You bitch; you have no right to order me, tell me what to do and what not to do anything. I own your ass here. It was DM's sympathetic love for you, that was coming in my way. However, now Raghav had crossed the limit."

"What did he do to give you this right?"

"He destroyed my factory in the Indian Ocean. That Bastard! Now I will show him. His Bhudevi's droid in every home. I have captured your sex routines. Every move you make. Everything you do. I've been watching you.

Yes, His wife's droid will be with every Tom, Dick and Harry. I will put up ads. Get a taste of royalty. He will suffer!"

"Ha Ha." Bhudevi laughed. "You think that will get you anywhere. You think that people doing it to a polysiliocon cylinder would equate doing it to me?"

"Polysilicon! Bitch! Wake up. Your skin and tissues have been captured. Within hours, I will have tissues made from stem cells and other internal organ cells that I am capturing here. And your internals will be replicated in every droid. Mass produced. A few billions down the drain. But what's money, in front of one's ego?

Every move, every twitch, every secretion will be proportionated to your exact actual responses. Ha Ha."

One droid gave her an anesthetic, and she was unconscious again.

Vibi had zoomed in onto the exact locations in mars.

"This large dome is the one where DM normally stays during his visits to Mars. SN, Kumb, Meghnath. all of them have bungalows alongside the beach. The few other buildings are research labs, staff quarters, various small model gardens and stuff like that.

These gardens are most advanced. The plants and trees are artificially made or biogenetically created. They can survive the cold and hot weather. The domes are made from multilayered complex petroplastic materials. There is some kind of gas flowing between the layers. They are also elastic. You could explode a bomb on top of these plastic-elastomers, and they would not crack open. And the gas would solidify and seal any cracks. The gas also has properties where their flow managed by electric currents produces quite an artistic show.

You have to find where Bhudevi is located first. Is she at this location?

The dome ends are where the gates are. It is quite difficult to locate these gates. However, look at long pipe like structures connecting different domes. These structures have multiple gates that can be sealed much like a submarine or ship, and each section can be compartmentalized."

Vibi zoomed in on one such structure. "See that side partition gate. You can enter a small helicopter through this gate.It is an engineering marvel." Vibi was quite proud. He had contributed to the design.

"The main dome connects to millions of domes a few kilometers in size, each with artificial lakes, gardens and what not based on the owner's preferences. Each sold for billions.

Some of them have been purchased by billionaires and sold to millions of upper-middle class people around the world for millions. It has created wealth around the universe."

It would be my first trip to Mars. I was securely strapped to the seat, as was Raghav. There was no steering and no controls from the hand available. It took off like a plane and in an hour's time we were in Mars. We were in touch with Lucky. Raghav had three communication satellites flying and covering mars. One of the few communication contracts that he had in Mars. He asked Lucky to have the satellites zoom in on DM's domes and see what could be found.

By the time they reached Mars, Lucky had struck gold. They saw someone jogging in a beach. They zoomed in and found it to be Bhudevi. Actually, it was not Bhudevi, but SN had made Bhudevi's droid practice the Bhudevi's jog sequence.

Raghav called the Galactic police office in Tholus and informed about Bhudevi's kidnapping and her location in Mars. They agreed to help him.

The chopper chosen was one of Raghav's choppers. It was small and could easily move in through the side gate. We were literally huddled in that confined space.

When Bhudevi woke up, she was in a hospital kind of environment. She felt a little weak. She must have been here for some time. It was DM's birthday today. She looked around. There was a Bhudevi droid. 'Moved here, to capture my movements, perhaps' she thought.

SharpNails walked in.

"So you are awake. Well, I have done it. Your internals are captured to the last exacting detail. Don't believe me. Move your fingers inside you and inside this droid. It will be exact.

It is DM's birthday today. So I will offer him, you. Frankly, after today, I wish that DM would release you. Release you to your world. You should see your shame. You should see Raghav ridiculed. Reduced to a shamed mortal.

However, DM is crazed about you. His ego is to have you. So I do not know."

Bhudevi understood that this woman had utilized DM's lust for her into her own profitable use. She had created a Droid empire based on one man's desire. She wanted to get up and slap SharpNails, but her arms and legs were moving in slow motion. SharpNails laughed at her and walked away.

Bhudevi started doing some pranayam and did kriya. That brought her some strength. She stood up from her bed and motioned for the Bhudevi droid to come and sleep in her place. The Droid followed her command.

No sooner had this happened; DM entered the room.

"I have given you enough time. Your time is up now. Raghav has failed to appear." He then looked at the real Bhudevi. Bhudevi started walking to the door making an accentuated robotic type motion with her arms and legs. "It is difficult to know, which is real and which the droid." DM laughed.

Bhudevi opened the door.

"Raghav has failed me. You are my true lover." The Droid said. "I should have realized your true love." Dialogues that SN had probably written for the droid. Spoken in a husky voice, that she used very rarely and only with Raghav.

That bitch (SN) was exact to a painful extent. Bhudevi walked out of the room and walked in the direction of the main door. She could see DM making love to the Droid behind her. There were video walls in the hall, all showing the DM making love to Bhudevi. The droid making the same sounds and motion that

Bhudevi used to make. SN had been exact to the minutest detail. Bhudevi felt sick.

She opened the main door.

A man was running towards her. He seemed familiar.

Was it Anjani? Yes!

He was followed by Raghav. Both of them and Lucky behind them were in their bullet-proof vests. They looked at her and at the video screens. DM making love to Bhudevi.

Raghav looked at Bhudevi. Bhudevi cried and held her arms up. Raghav realized that this was the real Bhudevi. They were followed by cops from the Galactic police.

The galactic police had already taken SN in their custody. SN was captured from her bungalow. They waited until DM finished his act and moved in to arrest him.

CHAPTER 12

I was back in a flight going to Earth. A very short trip to Mars. Raghav invited me and Suvi to Tholus, to be guests there.

Suvi was happy to have me back. It seemed ages that I had seen her. She started crying the moment, she saw me. Tears of joy. A late-night train to Bhimtal and we were on our holiday in Bhimtal.

We turned on the television set and saw some of the drama unfolding on TV.

The Galactic police had captured DM and brought him to the station in Tholus. His lawyers had already moved in there. The minimum press present in Mars also reached the Tholus station.

"What is DM arrested for?"

"Is it a part of the Indian Ocean incident?"

"Do you have any comment?"

"What are Bhudevi and Raghav doing here?"

"We have arrested DM on charges of Kidnapping Bhudevi and molestation of a woman." One policeman clarified.

"As you can see, the noted businessman DM, who was recently at the center of the controversy in the Indian Ocean, has also been arrested on charges of kidnapping and molestation. Keep watching Mars TV One'O'One for the latest developments."

Three channels were playing scenes from DM's building of his empire. From his earliest days, the different controversies, he had been in his lifetime, his Adult movie empire, his droid business run by SharpNails and other business that he owned.

Enough of this saga! I was sure that there would be some emails from Sugriv, informing me of the developments. We decided to walk to Jungaliya village and beyond. The hills are quite beautiful. During winter, you can see the snow-clad peaks of Nainital. Excellent view of the Naukuchiya tal or the Nine cornered lake.

The walk in the mountains put in a lot of fresh air into our system. We were energetic again for the next dose of each other.

Suvi turned on the TV again. She was as curious as me on the developments on the DM—SN—Raghav Bhudevi saga. It seemed that so was the whole world. It is not every day that you get to see royalty hurtling mud at each other.

A video of DM and Bhudevi's sex went viral. This was the latest thing that was being played on all news TV channels. People were seeing censored scenes from what I had seen during our rescue of Bhudevi.

"It was a Bhudevi droid and not Bhudevi." I clarified to Suvi. I told her bits and pieces of the story.

Bhudevi it seemed had already pressed Abduction and Rape charges against SN and DM.

"Are these allegations against DM and SN true?" Someone from the press, pressing a mike and seeking clarification from Bhudevi.

"No Comments. Since the matter is sub-judice, we will not be making any comments." Raghav was saying.

I checked my email. Sugriv had not sent anything.

Suddenly, the screen flashed with news. "DM Released."

I sent a message to Sugriv.

"What's going on?"

"Nothing. DM did not know that he was having sex with a droid. The moment he came to know of the same, his lawyers have issued a statement of false charges against Raghav and Bhudevi. But DM did not want to get released. That would make it mandatory to answer summons for the Indian Ocean incident.

They have, however, informed that Bhudevi had a signed contract with DM for acting in a movie and that all this was because of certain adult scenes in the movie. That Bhudevi's droid was used in these scenes and that since a droid was involved, there was no question of a Rape charge."

"What of the Indian Ocean Incident?" I asked.

"That is out of jurisdiction for the galactic police in Tholus. Raghav and Myself have done the media blitzkrieg on the Indian Ocean incident. We got hold of the many prisoners who have given written affidavits against SN corporation. However, someone from the Indian Ocean has to write to Interpol, and they have to transfer to the Galactic police and so on. That may take a long time.

Once the tide turned against DM, and people knew that they would not be minting money from DM, but there is a chance of making more money by claiming money by filing misuse suits against SN corporation, even those who were previously doing all these work wholeheartedly have turned against SN corporation."

"Anything else?"

"You were not here when the media blitzkrieg on the Indian Ocean was going on. Your name appeared in many news channels and newspapers.

Someone called Greg described you as the messenger from Raghav, who had created all this Havoc. Burnt down the evil empire of SN corporation. You were a hero among many of the released prisoners."

"I'm happy that you are happy."

What I did not know was that Raghav and Sugriv had executed a media blitzkrieg against the industrial abortion process in DM's islands. DM was portrayed as a dictator who did many evil things. DM's organization issued counter statements. However, the press was flying in choppers to the island in the Indian ocean and stories from the prisons in the islands flooded in. DM's organizations in many countries were besieged by angry people. People, who's loved ones worked in DM's organizations. People who hated him for various reasons, and rich people haters, all moved in. Many political and apolitical organizations tried to take advantage of this turn of events to damage DM's property's and DM's business. His image got dented beyond repair.

With SN and DM's arrest, the entire SN operations in the Indian Ocean went into a kind of limbo. The governments needed someone to take care of the dismantling and sale process. The shareholders were crying for DM's blood. Raghav had purchased a lot of shares for the shares of DM were being dumped by many investors. From 120 dollars a few days ago they came to 13 cents per share. He issued a statement and proposed that the successor for SN be named, and he chose Vibi.

Vibi in a press conference assured that the businesses that were causing hurt to the people would be dismantled. All operations would become ethical and be open for international inspection. The prisons would be dismantled. He would establish processes to see that such large-scale disruption of operations was impossible in the future. The stock price stabilized and rose to 1 dollar per share.

DM and SN knew that by having Vibi sworn in as the new president, Raghav had played a trump card. Their fates were sealed. They could not return to earth and face all those liability claims that were being laid out. They were kind of banished. The shareholders, employees and others crying for their blood.

I focused on the different things that I had planned with the Variable ramp, sometimes dressed in latex clothes, sometimes without them or the front opening stuff that Suvi had liked. We did some role plays too. We visited Bhimtal, Naukuchiya tal and Sat Tal during the daytime. We walked a lot and trekked the different mountains in the ranges there. We used the opportunity that nature provided us with to enjoy each other to the fullest extent. Nothing like some warm exercise in natural environments! Get my drift?

A petition was presented, explaining the incident starting from the signing of the movie by Bhudevi, to her eventual release from DM's home in Mars.

The petition that Bhudevi had written was very simple:

"I was hired by a protégé of Kumb to make a movie on Shakuntala. Since the Movie had a lot of fantasy elements, the set was made in one of the domed bungalow plots hired by the movie. Giant artificial plants and skies had to be made. This was possible using the exotic dome homes marketed by DM corporation.

I had been going to the set every day. A large part of the day was lost in making changes to the set. One day, some mysterious gas emanated from the A/C vent, and I was rendered unconscious.

On regaining Consciousness, I found that I was imprisoned in someone's home. DM has made a lot of movies about his love for me and his taking care of Droids made around me by SN. I was shown these during my captivity.

DM himself appeared and professed his love for me. I asked him to return me to my home in Tholus. He refused to do so. I was held captive wherein I learnt that DM, SN, Kumb and Meghnath were the different players who had hatched this plot to satisfy their boss DM's lust.

I was confident that Raghav would seek my release.

I also learnt that SN had been secretly capturing critical aspects of our body anatomy without our consent. The purpose of which was to make exact replica droids for the satisfaction of her boss.

I was forcibly drugged, and my internals examined for making such droids.

They also injected a Raghav like droid during my captivity, to capture my sex signature, again for satisfying the lust of her boss. And at a later date for mass production of such droids.

My modesty has been hurt. I request that the most stringent punishment be meted out to these criminals. By capturing my signature and my internals and replicating it on a droid and having sex with the droid, DM has committed rape.

Sd.

Bhudevi."

To which the Defendants replied as below:

"The allegations made by Bhudevi are all false. Bhudevi was signed to make a movie. She expressed consent to be in Mars and at the sets as required for the duration of the movie. Which, is still under production and not yet completed.

That there exist droids made on Bhudevi and other celebrities around the world is a known fact. That DM has a right to use such droids for his personal use is a right granted by the constitutions of the world and the Galaxy.

It has been acknowledged by Miss Bhudevi that DM has had sex with her droid and not with her. This is very much within the constitutional rights of DM and hence there is no question of a rape having been committed.

We, therefore, request that the case be summarily dismissed as all these allegations do not have any legal grounds."

It seemed that an interesting debate was brewing on TV. This was being widely followed by everyone on TV. It had the highest TRP's or viewer ship ratings. Frankly, the jury would have to go along with the general opinion in this case, or so it was felt.

The most discussed debate was on One'O'One Tv's 'Night with Amby' show.

It was an hour-long show. The debate here would give a shape for the case.

Amby invited the best scholars, legal minds, thinkers and philosophers and divided them into pro and con teams based on their individual biases.

Amby read out the petition from Bhudevi and the response to this allegation.

The Con team started the debate in a heated way.

"The Question is very simple. Do we as humans have a right to buy a droid modeled after anybody we desire in the world or not? I say that "YES" we have a right to buy a droid modeled after the best people in the world. This is our dream. This is what makes our life livable. That DM had a right to use the Bhudevi droid."

"You are talking about the right of DM, but what of Bhudevi's rights. She was forcibly kidnapped . . ."

"I object! Who says that she was kidnapped? She is the one claiming that. She has claimed many things, including a rape and also admitting that DM has only had sex with a Droid. She is a hypocrite."

"You are taking sides. The police have already acknowledged that there exists a ground to believe that Bhudevi could not escape the place without external help."

"The Police report also claims that Bhudevi had a signed contract with DM's organization to make the movie."

And so the debate went on. Amby correcting it and guiding it when they went out of limits.

A respected professor was also a part of the Con team. He spoke in a low voice, and he was respected for his opinions. His say would carry on to the minds of the Jury.

"My opinion is that DM is being incarcerated for becoming what he has become. A rags to riches story. Everyone wants to nail him down. This society does not want the people in rags to outgrow them. This has always been the case. Madam Bhudevi! You may be a model of virtue. You may have a live in relationship that most people think as a solid commitment but very few . . . madam very few believe in more than a night's commitment to another person. There are a million men and women available every night for experimentation and living. Where is the need for an individual to live with another for a lifetime? We have gone past this era. Wake up Bhudevi. You have opted to be in this business. To be famous and to be popular. We the people, have given you this, and we seek your secrets, your body in the form of a droid, so that we can live that dream that you portray on the screen. By not giving your body to us, you are denying us our right. You take our money, our praise, and yet you deem, your body equivalent being with us, as derogatory. Amby and respected jury of One'O'One TV, this woman thinks of herself as some royalty, bound to her King Raghav, looks down upon us common people with disdain. We are the ones that make you what you are madam, and we demand our pound of flesh."

There was a hefty applause. The Professor had spoken at the end and had expressed what the general populace had in mind. They had a right to their dreams. These celebrity droids were their ticket to a fantastic life that they saw in celebrity shows and the lives of the rich and famous people's shows.

The Jury in Amby's show voted that SN was guilty of kidnapping and droidizing Bhudevi. However, the Jury saw this as a debatable exercise. Bhudevi, in view of her being a popular public figure had a moral right to have willingly made her droid for the benefit of the universe. It was long overdue. That she had not done so was ground enough for someone to try all avenues possible to do so.

That the Jury found DM not guilty, and that he be discharged from this case and to be tried in the case in Indian Ocean incident.

I felt a bit sick. We were a disappearing breed. Suvi, Myself, Raghav, Bhudevi, Sugriv and his wife. While we were trying to revive marriage and some were looking at long-term relationships, the whole world was moving away from any commitment to a single person. Everyone was independent and free. There were a million men and women to have a relationship with, why tie oneself to one person and deny all others the opportunity of companionship?

I knew that the jury would vote more in lines with what had happened in Amby's show. The world was finding DM guilty of the Indian Ocean incident, but they had begun to have a sympathy for him in the Bhudevi incident. Almost all the women interviewed on

TV, were praising DM's love. They were a hysteria with women screaming.

"DM, Love me!"

"Abduct me DM!"

"Make love to me DM!"

You could see such frenzied and crazed women appear on TV every now and then.

To us, it seemed that sanity was coming to an end.

Emboldened with the tide turning in their favor, SharpNails granted an interview from her prison. She sat dressed in a plain professional attire. She probably looked like an executive in any of the thousands of organizations around the universe.

"Do you plead guilty to all these charges?"

"What Charges are we talking about. We are supposed to be in the expanded universe. We talk of our expanded consciousness. We talk of freedom. What is this freedom? What is this choice?"

"What of Bhudevi's freedom?"

"What about it? She chose freely to work in this movie. She chose to be away from her husband. She herself chose to have a Droid of her husband made. Why is the media not asking her, what she was doing in Mars?

She was in Mars, shooting for a movie. What is this Movie business but make believe?

What was she doing with a Raghav Droid? Why is nobody asking her this question?

She was fulfilling her fantasy with a man of her choice.

What about the choice of the Billions. Billions who spend their hard-earned money to see Bhudevi playing a role of Cinderella or Shakuntala. Billions who yearn to possess that body, that fantasy for a few moments. The fantasy that she is selling."

"But they would not have Bhudevi forcibly held up."

"All this idea of force is a myth. Bhudevi came on her own will. Nobody held her forcibly. Her main contention is a case of rape. And of copying her to make a Droid.

From time immemorial, people have been making statues of people they fantasize or people they love or of celebrities. Eklavya made a statue of Dronacharya and learnt to be a great archer. Look at Khajurao, so many people immortalized into statues making love. Today, a million men and women are employed in the Droid industry, making such walking idols for men, women who need companionship, who need their fantasies fulfilled.

What is a droid? It is a Scupltur that is moving, talking and doing things. Finally, it is an object.

This fight is not about Bhudevi. This fight is about the rights of those millions employed by this industry. Do they have a right to make a living statue? Nobody punished a sculptor in the past. The rocks in India's temples are live witnesses of that.

Nobody had cursed Khajuraho and its nude statues, but these morons with their debased opinion of what is right and what is wrong, want to punish the sculptor of today."

This passionate speech, which I felt could have been from a paid channel was being played in many TV channels. So many TV reporter's reporting:

"As you have just seen, that was SharpNails giving her part of the story. It is indeed a very valid point. Do those millions who are employed by the Droid industry have a right to make droids? Are the owners of the Droids rapists?"

Suddenly, the issue of AIDS was raked up.

"Before the droids came into popular existence, people were dying of diseases like AIDS, AIDS3 and other sexually transmitted diseases. When SN corporation made the droids with the auto flush sequence and cleaning in place droids, it has become very safe to have sex with a droid. Why are people forgetting this fact? Why has this not come up so far?"

I switched off the TV. We seemed to be losing the war. We had won a few battles, the rescue in Indian Ocean, the rescue of Bhudevi and yet the case seemed lost. DM and SN would be back and would find ways to regain their old stature. Vibi would probably be out of work, sacked unceremoniously. Vibi facing this ignominy twice in his career in a short span.

Our planned vacation was coming to an end. I thought of so many new things that we had discovered about each other. I had looked up a latex dressing store that I had discovered online, while Suvi had also become a bit bold and was scanning many leather stores online.

"Do you know that there are many leather dress stores in Agra and Delhi?"

"But they mostly make bags, dresses, sweaters."

"They also do some 'made to order' stuff."

"That's and idea. We need to locate someone who will do things of our choice."

"Don't ask me to come with you this time. I feel shy. You manage it on your own now."

"Yes M'lady! Your wish is my command!" I went on my knees and took her hand. We laughed some more.

And in all this, when we did get some time, we turned on TV. The same questions seemed to be going on:

What do Raghav and Bhudevi think? Do they want to throw us into the dark ages?

Who gave them a right to enforce this exclusivity, one man made for one-woman stuff?

Soon they will be promoting women as slaves to men.

These are super-rich people who are transgressing on our freedom.

I have a right to choose who I want to sleep with tonight.

Madam Bhudevi, You chose to be famous and to be a celebrity, and we demand your droid.

When you chose to be a public figure, you have a duty to make your details available.

The issue took a strange turn. SharpNails actually became a heroine. People idolized her as a pirate who had risked everything to help freedom of choice.

Raghav and Bhudevi were looked at as snooty rich folks, who chose to live an isolated life. Maybe they hated ordinary folks and considered themselves royalty.

Bhudevi's case of abduction and rape against DM was coming on trial in a week's time. There was an email from Sugriv, urging me to leave for Mars along with Suvi on Raghav's flight, all expenses paid. I was a material witness to the abduction and rape business.

So it looked like our holidays would extend.

The council of the world had many members on the jury board. It was the first time I had heard of this council. It was headed by someone named Wish. It was a 'hush-hush' organization of the movers and shakers of the world and galaxy. Wish had already met Raghav, and the process of his induction was being initiated. That is the reason Raghav was able to induct Vibi at the head of the organization. If Raghav considered it the big league, then it must be the biggest of the big leagues!

However, Raghav asked me to be very careful. DM had powerful people behind him. He also had a lot of politicians, bureaucrats in his pockets. SN had placed a security alert for me in SN corporation. This particular thing meant that key commando forces hired by SN corporation, had to seek me out and eliminate me in the easiest possible way. However, once Vibi took over the organization; he had removed the security threat alert that SN had placed. He had put me in the friend list or a list where every possible assistance was to be given to me. Costs would be borne by SN corporation.

I was moving up in life!!

CHAPTER 13

When I and Suvi arrived in Tholus, Raghav and Bhudevi were there to receive us. Raghav had many guest houses in Tholus, or should I say guest palaces. We were given one such guest house. The house had four master bedrooms, each designed like the best of different era's. An Amrapali suite, a Mughal suite, One a bedroom made in European palatial style, one was a pool with a floating bed on it. Each bedroom had royal clothes from that location era in its cupboard.

DM's movies had had a profound effect on society. Any ways, to us, it looked like our 'experimentation' holiday had just got extended.

We were all resigned to the tide going against us. Raghav had someone called Nadir advising him. They seemed cool.

The preliminary disposition would start the next day. Bhudevi requested that the media be kept away. SN and DM did not want the media to get involved. The media would question them about the Indian Ocean incident and sling some more dirt on their faces.

The press in the universe did not want the case to be dismissed summarily and neither did they want to be left out of it. They had petitioned to be present in the courts as the outcome of the case had implications on every human being in the universe. The stay on the presence of the press had to be removed. However, a restriction was placed on the press, and they would not be able to question or be a part of the process but be mute witness.

We were in the courtroom. DM and SN were already all smiles. The Amby show was more than half the battle. There was no way, this jury could go otherwise.

Bhudevi was called to the stand and asked to depose. She told her story as per her deposition.

"Objection My lords."

"On what grounds?"

"The witness is guessing that DM had put in the gas that supposedly made her unconscious. First, we do not know if there was a gas that came out or if Bhudevi had gone of her own will, or if she had taken some alcohol or drugs or frankly, plainly fell asleep. And she is conjecturing that DM had her drugged!"

"Sustained! The Jury may disregard Bhudevi's remark that DM had had her drugged in the makeup van."

I was astounded. Certainly, this injection of gas was part of DM and SN's plot. However, the legal world is a stupid world. They did not believe Bhudevi. Bhudevi was taken aback. She had not guessed that someone would question her story.

She continued her story and the defendant's lawyers also objected to her being in captivity.

"We would like to cross examine this statement now. Before Miss Bhudevi makes more accusations that will get registered in the Jury's mind."

"That is preposterous. You will get your time." Our Lawyer interrupted.

"My lord. We need to ask Bhudevi, if she was tied or chained in the period she claims that she was a captive."

"Were you restrained in any manner?" The Honorable judge asked.

"No My lord. There was no need. The whole place is so remote, that there is no possibility of anyone moving out."

"My Lord, I think that Bhudevi thought that she was being held captive. Like in a movie. However, she was actually a free woman, free to leave as she wished. That she had signed a contract, not withstanding, she claims to have been kidnapped. It should be noted that she chose to be there. She was jogging, enjoying the artificial sky, probably swimming and tanning in a beach. My lord, may the Jury be made to note that she was not tied or chained or handcuffed, but that she chose to remain in these premises. As per her contract!" The last sentence was a punch line.

"Sustained. The Jury may note that she was not chained or tied or restricted in any manner. But the Jury may also note that the place was very remote."

Things were not looking very good for us.

The Defendants decided that cross examinations would happen later as required. So Raghav was made to come to the stand.

He told his side of the story. That he had sent me on a mission to the Island in the Indian Ocean.

"Mr. Raghav, you had two droids made. One of Bhudevi and one made as yourself."

"Yes."

"What was the purpose?"

"It was to be our conduit to each other."

"Meaning, you could physically connect to each other via this Droid."

"It was not entirely like that."

"Mr. Raghav, I do not have the same sensibilities like you, and I may find it difficult to understand, so I will ask a 'Yes' or 'No' answer from you. Did you and/ Or Bhudevi ever have a physical relationship with this droid?"

"Yes, but we had the other person always available at the other end."

"I really do not understand, why that makes any difference. However, I will take your answer to mean 'Yes'.

Honourable Judge and members of the jury, see the hypocrisy here. We have two of the leaders in our society, one, an actress par excellence and a businessman talking about the evil things about having sex with a droid. And they own droids of their own for their own satisfaction, or should I say, own physical satisfaction.

They take millions from ordinary people and become richer. However, these same ordinary people cannot have droids made for them and are denied a right to satisfy their desires. What hypocrisy!

Now may I ask you to see the woman in row 3, just behind Bhudeviji."

Everyone turned around. It was a Bhudevi droid.

He motioned to the droid. The Droid got up. He motioned the droid to sit in a chair.

"See this Droid. This is not Miss Bhudevi. This is the droid that DM had sex with. Just like any of us, including the esteemed Mr. Raghav here, has had experience with Droids, this is a droid."

The arguments closed for the day. Raghav did not appear distraught. Was I missing something?

"You can do so much. Then it is destiny." He had said once, when he was helping Sugriv. It looked like all was lost. I did not see the Jury upholding the Rape charge, neither could we decisively prove that Bhudevi was abducted.

We were playing hide and seek that evening. I had to guess which bedroom we would be using. The loser was to be blindfolded and tied to the bed. The other person had five whole minutes to play with the tied person. I checked the room with the floating bed. I was right. Suvi was there.

"Oh! No" Suvi said.

"Oh! Yes!"

We decided to go for a walk after dinner. We walked out. There seemed to be some activity in the main building or shall I say main palace.

"Let's check what's going on." I said.

We walked in and found Raghav, Bhudevi, Lucky, Sugriv and a few others huddled around a Holographic TV projector. They acknowledged our presence, but focused on what was going on.

Mars One'O"One was showing a big container in the Island, that I had accidentally damaged (or parts of the island at least). The whole garbage container was filled with waste organic materials from the abortions that were being carried out. The TV reporter showing the garbage can and describing the 'abortion' operations. This was followed by an animated presentation of the abortion process. It all looked gruesome. The container caused a nauseating sensation. I felt that I was going to puke. Luckily, the TV reporter started showing the burning diesel tank and other scenes.

The reporter then went ahead and described the hero of the whole episode, i.e. myself.

"This is happening at a good time." I said. "At least the Jury will know that they are not dealing with heroes or Robinhood's. These guys are rotten to the core."

"Thank you Nadir." Raghav thanked Nadir.

Next day when we reached the courthouse, we learnt that Vibi had located and provided tapes from the surveillance videos from DM's home in Mars.

The Honorable Judge started:

"We have also received tapes and video's from SN corporation, authenticated by its new President Mr. Vibi. Which corroborate most of what Miss Bhudevi has said. Except that there is clear evidence that DM had sex with the Droid, and the Droid invited DM to have sex. I have arranged for the videos to be demonstrated. The press may not capture any of this. Bailiff, please arrange for all Camera's to be outside."

For the next few hours, we saw the trauma that Bhudevi went through. Many hours of video recording were fast forwarded. Only times when DM entered and there were dialogues, were seen. There was evidence of

SN talking derogatorily with Bhudevi and then there was evidence that DM had sex with the droid.

I was put on the docks next.

I told the story of my involvement with this incident. The point of interest being my visit to the Indian Ocean island. I recounted the story of captivity in the Indian Ocean. The press had been very vociferous in stating that the Island was so remote that no one in his sane mind could escape. I was seen as an ordinary person on a job. Though I was given some perks, I was still a commoner. My viewpoint was taken as the viewpoint of a commoner.

"Do you agree that you sabotaged the Diesel tanks?"

"No My lord. It was an accident caused by the tampering done to the Jet Pack by SN corporation." One of the guards had already accepted doing this on DM's behest. This already was shown on TV.

I described DM as a megalomaniac, a person with a mindset of being a king or a ruler and how he had transgressed on ordinary people's lives. The group's now known industrialization of abortions for stem cells was also a pain point for many people. I reminded them of the abortions. Last evening's TV report was fresh in everyone's mind.

The Judge asked me on what I found in Mars.

"Do you think that the droid objected?"

"Sir, the Droid was programmed not to object. Had it been programmed otherwise, it may have objected."

"So it cannot be classified as a rape."

"My lord, I am a small person and have limited knowledge of Droids. I have never used them. But what is Rape? When a person forces another person to have sex by force or by intimidation then it is Rape.

I have seen movies where men chase a woman and then they force themselves upon her. The availability of droids, makes it unnecessary to have forced sex.

What differentiates a person from another? By capturing my signature, my responses, when a person is having sex with a droid made from these responses, then it is as good as having sex with me. That is the premise under which SN corporation is selling these Droids.

When they sell a droid of a celebrity, they claim that they have captured everything that is the celebrity. Everything, including organ size, its throbbing frequency, its secretion quantum, time, style of sex, noises, everything that is the celebrity.

If the celebrity has consented to capture these signatures, then it is sex.

If I have a personal relationship with the person owning my Droid, it could even be love.

But if it is forced or done by piracy, then it is rape. As good as someone catching a girl and doing it forcibly."

"Hmnn . . ." The Judge went. "It is an interesting viewpoint. Thank you Mr. Anjani."

EPILOGUE

I did not know that we were in the center of a drama affecting the entire universe. What had happened was drawing in so many varied reactions and effects around the world and human inhabited galaxy.

The jury found DM and SN conspirators in abducting Bhudevi. SN was also guilty of forcibly capturing Bhudevi's sexual signatures and incorporating in a droid. They ordered that such droids made without the will of Bhudevi be confiscated and destroyed. They did find DM guilty of Rape.

DM and his lawyers were definitely going to go to higher courts for a reversal of decision.

The court case did cause a scare among pirated droids.

But they found workarounds, where the pirates would incorporate one visible feature that was different than the celebrity and claim that the droid was not of that celebrity. People held demonstrations against this perceived censorship.

The case was over, but both sides of the debate kept debating, over emails, chats and other media.

Raghav it was rumored had made it big in the hush-hush organization. Raghav and Bhudevi decided to marry and convert their Live-in to a marriage.

And we found a Leather handicraft store in Mumbai, ready to make the latex type dresses in leather for us.